CHLOE

CHLOE

JONATHAN BROWN

LEVEL
BEST BOOKS

Author Photo Credit: Sonia Brown

First edition

ISBN: 978-1-68512-142-6

Cover art by Level Best Designs

This book was professionally typeset on Reedsy.
Find out more at reedsy.com

I dedicate this book to all who have suffered at the hands of an abuser. Get out. Get help. Stay strong. It's not your fault!

Praise for CHLOE

"Chloe Savannah takes no prisoners. Armed with a five-and-a-half-inch Colombia River stainless steel knife and a 4.0 GPA, Chloe is out to get the bad guys threatening her sheriff in Bucksville, California in this fast-paced and deftly written novel from Jonathan Brown. A page turner that will keep you reading and applauding Chloe's bad ass behavior right to the end."—Cathi Stoler, author of The Murder On The Rocks Mysteries

"Brown's first stab at a female protagonist hits the bullseye in CHLOE, a complex crime-filled coming-of-age tale that pulls no punches. When your best friends are the knives strapped to your body, or slipped under your pillow, there's not much the world can throw your way that you can't handle. But don't feel sorry for this young killing machine from Bucksville, cheer her on—from a safe distance."—Linda Sands, Georgia Author of the Year, *3 Women Walk Into A Bar*, The Cargo Series

"Bronze, brainy, and beautiful, Chloe's also about the deadliest 17-year-old you'll ever come across. She's hard to stop and even harder to scare. Knives are her jam, and you want to think twice before you get on the wrong side of Chloe—or her friends. Everyone could use a friend like Chloe."—SJ Rozan, bestselling author of *Family Business*

"Chloe is smart, sometimes vulnerable, and always tough; and if you're in trouble you want her on your side."—Terry Shames, author of the Samuel Craddock series

Chapter One

I t was a totally vivid dream because it was about something that had happened to me, not long ago. He had long greasy hair that flowed over pointy, broad shoulders. His teeth were yellow-brown. The ones he had anyway. I don't know how Momma could have kissed that mouth, let alone do anything else with the pig. I was sick to my stomach at the sight and smell of him. Momma always brought home drunks, but this one smelled not only of cheap booze, but of days if not weeks since a bar of soap had been anywhere near his emaciated body.

I hated Momma in those moments—loathed, actually.

They'd kept me up all night with their disgusting pleasure sounds. I thought drunks were supposed to do it once and then pass out. Oh well.

Fuck my life.

The next day I was at the sink filling up the coffee pot when he slid in behind me, reached around, and grabbed my tits.

"Whoa! Fuck off!" I said, throwing my head backwards. It connected with his chin and bottom lip. He wiped the blood with the back of his hand. His sinister laugh cut like barbwire down my spine.

"What the hell's going on?" Momma came out of the bedroom with a ton of sleep in her eyes. I didn't bother answering. She knew damn well what happened. It always happened. Greasy hair ignored Momma as well. She moved to him, looking for a kiss or hug. Any form of affection that said he loved her...at least for now. Instead, he came at me again. This time I had Norma Jean out of the scabbard and in my hands. He came in with arms outstretched and hands aiming for my face. Or maybe my throat, who

1

knows?

I side-stepped and brought my blade across and down. He screamed as the tips of three fingers tumbled into the sink. With his good hand, he clutched the injured one and called me all kinds of names. Even threatened to kill me. Momma unleashed an unintelligible litany of shit before she read the thought in my eyes. Mothers can do that. She hustled to the sink, but I hip-checked her out of the way. She stumbled forward, colliding with her lover. I got to the sink and looked back at them.

I shoveled the fingertips into the disposal hole and stood with my hand on the switch.

"No, please don't, honey," he whimpered. "I'm sorry, I—"

With a giant smile, I said, "Whoopsie!" I then flipped on the garbage disposal. Greasy hair howled, "No!" And ran to the sink. I leaped out of the way. He turned off the disposal, but we all knew he was too late.

"Sucks to be you...Stubby," I said. Momma put her face in her hands and cried.

Useless.

The greasy bastard motioned like he was coming for me. With legs bent, I swung Norma Jean back and forth in tight figure-eights. I said nothing, but my face urged him to try me. His face twisted and contorted as he considered his options. Blood seeped through the fingers of his good hand. He glanced at the crimson pool forming at his feet.

"Ya better run along, Stubby," I said.

He hesitated a moment. Momma kept crying.

"You crazy bitch!" He said and bolted out the front door. His truck roared to life, and he was gone. The dream went wacky after that. Suddenly I was drowning—suffocating actually, in a room full of bloody fingertips.

I bolted upright. My tank top was covered in sweat. And my heartbeat pounded in my ears. Slowing my breathing, I eased Norma Jean from beneath my pillow and kissed the five-inch blade near the serrated portion.

Good girl.

Chapter Two

I poked my head in Momma's room, knowing she'd still be asleep. Then I peed and brushed my teeth. Before showering or breakfast, I headed outside and did my morning workout. I stretched, did push-ups and squats, and then I got down to business. Here is where I'll clue you into Norma Jean. As you know, that was Marilyn Monroe's real name. And yes, I'm obsessed with her. Everything about her.

On my hip in a worn leather sheath is Norma Jean, the knife. She's crafted by the Colombia River Company and has a five-and-a-half-inch blade. Two and a half inches are serrated on the top side of the stainless steel. My obsession with Marilyn Monroe is equaled by my love for knives. It's my thing. And one of the many things that make me different from most high school seniors in my group.

I wore a thin cotton t-shirt, loose cargo pants for mobility, and my black Wolverine boots. With the warm up done, I move on to tossing my knife. I toss knives with both hands for hours on end. And although I'm only seventeen, I'd bet I've spent more than the ten thousand hours that Anders Ericsson introduced, and was later made more popular by Malcolm Gladwell.

I've got an old stump I use for low tosses and an array of old fence posts set at different heights for the higher throws. Momma thinks both me and the habit are crazy. She may be right, but I don't care. I practice over-hand throws, underhand, side arm, and standing off balance. Hang on. I'm not done. I toss on the run, diving, in and out of tumbling, and even backward throws. I even set up cans, usually Momma's empty beer cans, and pick them off. If macho dudes shoot tin cans with handguns, why can't I throw knives at them? The routine usually lasts anywhere from a minimum of forty-five minutes to an hour and a half or more. With an even sheen of sweat on my body, I'll hit the shower next.

Momma was still asleep when I came in. At least she didn't have a 'guest' over so I could shower in peace. I'm not claiming her drunk 'friends' storm in on me with regularity, but I'd be lying if I said it hasn't happened, and I mean more than once.

Sick bastards.

I'm always stoked when strangers aren't around on the days when I wash my hair. Being of mixed race—Momma's white, daddy was black, my hair is part afro and part blond-girl ringlet. And the shit is long. I love my hair (and I'm not the only one), but it's a bitch to maintain. I've got more shampoos, conditioners, relaxers, softeners, straighteners, moisturizers, strengtheners, and detanglers than any hair salon on the west coast. And that's just the hair products.

Even though Momma didn't have a friend over doesn't mean one of her past stray dogs wouldn't come sniffing around. So, I not only lock the bathroom door, I keep Norma Jean on the rack that hangs off the shower head. The rack barely hangs onto the metal head. I need to replace it, like so many things around the house—more like trailer—but I keep forgetting. I bet you're worried about rust on Norma Jean. Don't be. I keep her in a freezer bag, and even after that, I wipe her down.

It takes me about twenty minutes to wash, condition, and rinse my hair. If Momma gets up and has to pee, tough shit. I don't unlock that door until I'm dressed, and Norma's back on my hip.

I do a combination of blow-dry and towel dry, so add another twenty minutes to the whole routine. When I'm done and dressed, the hair has its natural curl, almost ringlets, like I said earlier, and hangs to about the bottom of my shoulder blades. Makeup is minimal. With my smooth mocha skin color and naturally long lashes, which accent my blue-gray eyes, I honestly don't need much. Sound like a brag? Don't care. It is what it is. I get hit on, a lot, by both male and female. Sadly, I get hit on the most by older men. Older men that not only should know better, they *do* know better and they don't give a shit. They're up for it and hope I am as well. And why always the married ones? Fucking gross!

* * *

I got my ass to school and decided to blow off the last class, P.E. I just washed my hair, for god's sake. O'Donnell, the bitch P.E. teacher who hates me because she has a thing for Mr. Clancy tells me I need to go see principal Cross if I'm going to cut class. Mr. Clancy is the shop teacher who smiles at me way too often and looks at me a little longer than he should. And by the way, I don't even take Clancy's shop class!

Mr. Cross's secretary smiled and told me Mr. Cross was waiting for me. I knocked once and poked my head in.

"Mr. Cross, you wanted to see me?" I said. I loaded my voice with all kinds of sugar.

"Oh, come on in, Chloe. Everything alright? I just got off with Ms. O'Donnell."

I bet you did.

I decided not to sit down. I wasn't going to be staying long. "Mr. Cross, I have to skip P.E. today. I need to get home."

Principal Cross was a good guy, sweet actually. He put both thick-fingered hands on his desk and let out an exaggerated sigh. A speech was coming. Still, I didn't sit—not wanting to encourage the talk. He stood up and ran a hand over his head the way most people do when they have a full head of hair. He obviously missed his.

"Chloe, would you mind closing the door? Well, not closing it all the way, just sort of—"

"Ajar, Mr. Cross?" I smiled. He blushed slightly.

"Yes, ajar. Look, Chloe, you can't keep getting these absences. I know you're in your final year, and the finish line is in sight, but you need the hours."

His eyebrows formed a funny sort of upside-down V of concern. He really was a sweet guy.

"Wow, you sure seem to know a lot about my high school career. More than Ms. Mackenzie."

Mackenzie was my guidance counselor. Mr. Cross's cheeks flushed again. "Aw knock it off Chloe," he said coming around his desk to lean against the front of it. He crossed one ankle over the other and folded his arms over his skinny chest. I decided to take the chair.

"I know it's your mother. And it's real commendable you looking after her and such, but your mother made her choices. I'm sad for her and sorry for you that she's taken to liquor like she has." He paused. When he spoke again it was a whisper. "But *you* can't stop livin.'"

He was right. He pissed me off, but he was right. But that's my momma he was talking about. Drunk or not.

"I'm having my period and I don't have any tampons. I don't want to mess up your gymnasium floor, so—" It was a cruel shot but I get that way sometimes—a defense mechanism I suppose.

"Goodness gracious Chloe you can't talk like that, not in here," Cross said. He retreated back behind the safety of his desk. He wore a look of a kid who'd just walked in on his parents doing it. It really was a cheap shot.

"I'm sorry." A long silence passed. Mr. Cross fiddled with just about everything on his desk but his telephone. I twirled a thick lock of hair in my hands.

"Look, Chloe, I was, sorry, *am* quite fond of your mother. She used to be the happiest woman in all o' Bucksville. And she couldn't have been more proud when you came along."

The top of my head began to heat up. I could feel my lip start to quiver. I bit down hard on it to stop. No way was I going to cry in Cross's office.

"You know your parents were real happy in the early days. And if not for that damn war—"

Mr. Cross paused. The silence made it harder to hold back the tears, so I gave up trying. I let them come and felt bad about it because sweet Mr. Cross didn't know what to do.

"Jeez, Chloe, I'm sorry I didn't mean to—here, here's some uh, tissue. Can I get you some water?"

I took the tissue and forced the end of the flow. "No, I'm fine. Thanks for being so friggin' nice, Mr. Cross."

"Alright, alright, but ya watch your language, ya hear?"

Mr. Cross went back to fidgeting while I gathered myself. I needed to get out of that office, but I didn't want my peers seeing me like this.

"I gotta go. For all I know, Momma's choking on her sick right about now."

"But Chloe—"

"Oh, oh," I said. I looked down at my jeans fly. "I think it's about to happen, Mr. Cross."

"Mother of pearl—jeez, Chloe…."

I opened the door and turned back to Mr. Cross, who wore a huge sympathetic look on his face.

"Thanks, Mike."

"Ah, it's Mr. Cross, young lady. And you're welcome. Good luck."

Chapter Three

It wasn't really true what Mr. Cross said. I really don't need the hours. I'm rocking a 4.0 GPA and I'm blessed that I maintain it with very little effort. But Cross has given me at least a half-dozen lectures over time about setting a good example for the other students. Like they give a shit about mine or anyone else's attendance. Cross is just from a different time—god love the little boomer.

I like leaving school early before the mad rush of kids all trying to escape the jail at the same time. I'm tired of hearing about all of the great plans and potential hook-ups of the mean girls with the hotties. Just as much as I'm over all the whistles and cat-calls from the jocks. I've been here for four years, enough already.

Call it a curse or call it a blessing but I'm what is considered attractive. Hot actually. Now, I know that sounds boastful but it's not. I look at it as a genetic lottery—luck of the draw. I've got nicely shaped C-cup breasts, which arrived in the ninth grade. My body is naturally curvy—like a certain former blond starlet I'm obsessed with—and I keep it in shape. That means when I was a kid I looked weird but as a fully developed teen, I'm suddenly exotic. *Puke.* I don't know who sets these rules; wish I knew.

Being hot…blessing or curse? You tell me. I had very little to do with my look. My mother was a beautiful woman who's plopped down on the ladder to 'attractive' thanks to alcohol consumption, and my father was a handsome devil. The pictures don't lie.

I walked down 7th street, which parallels main. It's my usual route. Technically Main street is faster but 7th has more of the smaller shops that

I like. Plus, one side practically butts up against Eagle's Peak. Bucksville, California's highest mountain. It's truly a sight to behold. It's been shot from at least a dozen different angles and turned into postcards for the tourists, when postcards were a thing. Now it's all brochures and websites. Production companies often roll into town from L.A. to shoot movies. They never use our town's real name mind you, but we locals don't care. We sort of like our best kept little secret. Although, the secret seems to have been leaked, and the fucking tourists flood this place from March to September.

As I walked down the wide road I said a handful of hellos to various town-folk. Bucksville's a friendly place for the most part and just about everybody behaves peaceably.

When I got to Saul's Bakery I ducked in and was hit by the familiar pitch of the door chime. Saul was behind the counter with his skinny arms, legs to match, and huge belly pushing out the sides of his dirty apron. He had a smile like a five-year-old boy. He waited a beat before speaking. I closed my eyes and inhaled deeply. This was my ritual. I love the smell of a good bakery. Sugar, cinnamon, possibly nutmeg, and a host of other delicious odors graced my nostrils. Quenched, I slowly opened my eyes.

"Well, well, little Miss Chloe's early today. Tell me, hon', what are you *not* going to buy today?" It was our little routine. He wasn't really angry. But he was right. I rarely buy anything. I just love the smell of a good bakery.

"Hey Saul, I know, I'm sorry, but I stop here almost every day, and if I bought something every time I'd be three hundred pounds inside a month."

"And you'd still be a pretty girl so what's the problem?" Saul pretended to be serious knowing full well I wasn't shopping. Still, we had to keep up the back and forth.

"Easy now, Saul I'm still an innocent, impressionable high school senior."

Saul's nephew Little Danny snickered as he pushed his broom across the floor. Saul had mild panic in his eyes.

"Hey, hey," he said raising his hands in retreat, "Saul is a happily married man, don't make this awkward."

"Just teasing ya Saul. I know you're a good man. Maybe I'll buy something tomorrow."

"Saul will not hold his breath because it's always tomorrow with you."

I mussed Little Danny's hair as I walked by. He snickered some more. At the door, I turned back to Saul.

"Saul needs to drop the third person act."

"Ah, see," he said, pointing at me, "there you go talking all brainy again. Like you're better than us blue-collar bakers."

"Your collar's white, Saul," I said. "But you're right, I am better than you."

We shared a laugh. "But I'm not better than Little Danny here." I mussed his hair a second time then tickled him. He dropped the broom and laughed hysterically. Little Danny is a low-functioning fifteen-year-old, but way smarter than everyone thinks.

"Have a good night, boys."

"You too Chloe," Saul said. "I hope you're mother's ok."

That's one of the problems with a small town like Bucksville; your business is everyone's business. At least I didn't have to try and conceal Momma's affliction; there was that I suppose.

As I stepped out of the bakery I saw my friend Shayna across the street riding her rusty-beige American thoroughbred heading in the direction I'd come from. Now don't go thinking Buckville's all dirt roads and tumbleweeds cause it's not. We've got paved streets like cities do; still, it's not uncommon to see people riding in town.

"Hey Shay-Shay," I called.

"Hey, Chloe. You're out early today."

"Yeah, duty calls." She knew I was referring to Momma. Shayna and I were real close when we were kids. She taught me how to ride in fact. We're still good friends but with me at the high school and Shayna home-schooling we don't hang out as much. I'm hoping that will change after graduation...that is if I'm still here in this town.

"Rusty's looking good, girl."

"Yeah, he's healthy, alright. Hasn't lost one bit of nasty, though. I gotta watch him like a hawk."

"Nah, he's a good boy," I teased. He threw me once when I was young but I was ready for it so I wasn't hurt. I got right back on him too. After that we were fine with each other. I could actually say he's my buddy.

"You want him? I'll give you a good price," she laughed.

"Careful girl he understands you, ya know."

Shayna clicked and picked up her pace. "Come by for a ride sometime, it's been a while."

"I'll take you up on that, Shayna. Thanks."

"Say hi to Momma for me, ya hear?"

Shayna was the only person other than me to call her that. It broke Shayna's heart when Momma took the turn. I was pissed at first because Shayna stopped coming by the house. I came to understand it later, though. She doesn't have the backbone that I have; she couldn't take Momma's change.

Once I cleared town, I took highway 11 toward my neighborhood. My house may as well have been a motor home. It was pretty much the same size, same layout right down to the flimsy front door and rusted siding. Only thing is she didn't have wheels under her. That meant that Momma and I weren't going anywhere; not anytime soon anyway.

Although I don't know how long alcoholics live—never looked it up. If Momma died soon, then I'd be gone the very next day. In that case, I *would* be going somewhere soon. I know that sounds cold, but I'm not. Not down deep anyway. But my momma chose to turn to liquor, which means she's given up on life. Giving up on life is darn near dead, isn't it? Either way, there's not much I can do for my mother other than take care of her. And that's exactly what I do. I'm Chloe, the committed; you can count on Chloe, that's me.

Momma was asleep on the living room couch when I walked in. 750 milliliters of Wild Turkey was two-thirds empty on the coffee table. Beside that were three empty Coors lite tall cans; momma's version of sidecars, I guess. This consumption was typical for her on a Friday.

The t.v. was on with the volume low. Momma does that when sleep comes on—if she remembers. I paced quickly to the kitchen to check the stove. I breathed a sigh of relief as all four nobs were in the off position. Our deal was no stove unless I'm home. She held up her end today; pretty good for a Friday. I checked the microwave, which she's allowed to use, and found an unmolested frozen mini pizza inside. A quick check with my hand told me she'd placed it inside and forgotten to turn on the microwave—the pizza was still frozen.

"Great, so you haven't eaten today, then." I didn't expect her to answer. I often talk to her when she's asleep—not sure why. I would have liked to have tossed the pizza, but we're not exactly in the tax bracket where we could throw food away. With Momma not eating today at least now I could feed her a healthy dinner instead of the empty-calorie pizza.

I returned the pizza to the freezer and tidied up. Aside from her empties and our breakfast dishes, the place wasn't too bad. My mother wasn't too messy on her own but get one of her gentlemen callers over here and all bets are off. I need to back up a moment. I shouldn't refer to any of her boyfriends as gentlemen. Very few of them have ended up on that side of the ledger.

Momma's got a pattern that she rarely strays from. After a few weeks on her own, she becomes lonely. She'll clean herself up, apply makeup, and do her hair. The 'killer dress,' as she often says, comes next. With the near-full beauty of her youth returned, she heads downtown to one or both of her two favorite bars: The Barn Door or The Brass Rail. That's where momma makes a friend. *Gross.* The new guy comes over and stays a few days, which is always when my life becomes hell on earth.

As I said, my mother's suitors were not Nobel Peace prize candidates. They're usually blue-collar guys, dumb as all get-up. On top of that, they were usually pissed at the world, and we all know half the world is made up of women. They were always temps, on their way somewhere or working temporarily in town. I straight-up dislike a man that hasn't settled down roots. It means whatever sort of trouble he stirs up he can simply pick up one day and piss off down the road. He ain't no different from a hurricane that touches down, then moves on. A man that's settled has accountability; he's got to otherwise society deals with him. At least that's how I see it.

When I look back at the long line of Momma's men, they remind me of stray dogs. I just wish we could be like the S.P.C.A. and tend to them the way the agency does at the end of their stay and put them down.

There's that cold Chloe again.

But I come by my chilliness honestly because I get no peace when they come around. In the eyes of the wandering loser, I'm the younger high school version of Momma. They look at me as the cherry on top of their Joselyn—that's Momma's name— parfait. They ogle, they stare, they brush up against me, and eventually, they make their play. I always beg Momma to take up with a local guy who's got his own place and move in with him. I'd love that, but no such luck.

Still, a girl can dream. I've become pretty handy thanks to Youtube 'how to' videos. I'm not quite a carpenter, but I'll get there. I'm no plumber either, but I can handle the minor household stuff. If Momma moved out, I'd put a real spit shine on this place…and then sell it and put this shit behind me. But as long as the moron circus continues to come through, there ain't no point in me fixing up anything. Too many drunken evenings in the past have torn down whatever I've built.

I'm sad to say that there's been more than one occasion when one of my mother's strays comes sniffing around my bedroom door when Momma's asleep. If they get too close, I introduce them to Norma Jean.

James Bond keeps a pistol under his pillow. I keep trusty Norma under mine, and I'm lethal with her. That I *will* brag about. Every night after supper and on weekends, I head outside and work my targets. I spend an hour minimum with both hands; hundreds of knife throws. I can comb a horsefly's hair from thirty feet, and he don't even half to sit still for it. *Booyah!*

I do more than toss my knife around. I also make tiny woodcarvings. I escape when I carve. My mind goes wherever she wants to go, which is usually anywhere but Bucksville. I realize I painted a quaint little *aw shucks* picture of Bucksville earlier, and that's all true. But it's the reality of life, my life, that has me yearning for change. I picture myself on the other side of the world and wonder what I'd be like and what I'd do. I picture handsome foreigners asking my hand in marriage, but I turn them all down…at first anyway. A girl needs to learn the lay of the land first. I want to taste the food, get to know the people, and speak the language. Yup, the language is a must because ain't no way I'm going to get into an argument with my fiancée and

13

not understand what the hell he's hollering about.

Momma stirred on the couch. "Hey, baby, when did you get home?"

"Fifteen minutes ago or so."

"Aw, and you let me sleep."

"I'm very good to you, Momma, you know that."

"Smartass," she yawned. "True, but you're still a smartass."

She sat up and ran her hands through her thick blond hair. Women all over town envied Momma's locks—thick, long, with a natural sheen and not a speck of gray in it. She arched her back and did a stretch. Her C-cups were as perky as mine. It was so sad she wasted her body on losers in bars. She looked down at her burgundy painted toes and smiled. She looked around the table and even peeked under it.

"I cleaned up your empties already, Momma," I said, pissed.

"Oh, are you sure they were all empty because—"

I rolled my eyes. She looked like she'd lost her favorite Barbie doll. *Pathetic.*

"Goin' out tonight? Or staying in with me to watch a movie?" My tone carried a slight edge with the second part of my question. I couldn't help it.

"What time is it?"

There was my answer. She was going off to act like a name a daughter shouldn't refer to her mother as. I got annoyed. "Does it matter what time it is?"

"Please, let's not do this, Chloe. I just woke up."

"Oh yes, that's right from your strenuous day of..." I paused to load up the sarcasm. "Drinking, was it? Oh, wait, it was drinking *and* sleeping."

"There she is, judge and jury, my daughter who's better than everybody else."

"Not everybody, just you, Joselyn." Momma hated it when I called her that. I do that when I'm pissed at her. She gave me the hard look only mothers and drunks can deliver. Maybe I deserved it. Still...don't care.

I went back to the freezer and pulled the pizza out, and stuck it in the microwave. When it chimed, I said, "Dinner's ready." I ditched my plan of making her a healthier meal. Petty and passive-aggressive? Sure, but I don't give a damn. I left her and went to my room for Norma Jean.

"Let me guess, you're going for that damn knife. You know, other girls your age are out on dates or hanging with friends. They sure as hell aren't throwing knives at posts."

I came back with Norma. She was in her sheath. I held her at my side. "No, Momma, girls my age are in backseats of cars with older college guys going all the way with them. You know why? So the creeps will love them. Be glad your daughter knows that ain't how love works." I headed for the door. "Or do I need to run the list down of single mothers my age at my school?"

"You're so damn melodramatic," Momma said, running her hands through her hair.

"Tina Johnson, remember her? Yeah, well, she's pregnant, *sixteen* and pregnant. I could go do that. Ya wanna be a grandma, Joselyn? Do ya?" I slammed the flimsy door on my way out. I'd barely cleared the bottom step when I let Norman Jean go. Fifteen yards away, she slammed into the fence post. She sunk in deep. I had to wiggle her around to get her out. I came and sat on the bottom step, pulled out my stone, and gave Norma a good sharpening.

"Bitch," I said. "She better not make a friend tonight!"

Chapter Four

I'd been asleep about an hour when they came in. The soundtrack was always the same. Stumbling, giggling, something knocked over, and then sex sounds coming from Momma's room. If there's a fine line between love and hate this is when I hated her. The day I graduate, I'm on a bus going anywhere. I've said it before but I never meant it because of school, but that would change in two months.

As the horrendous sounds penetrated my door and thin walls I asked myself if I'd been helping my mother all this time or enabling her? I asked my guidance counselor once when I was in the tenth grade. She gave me a very vague answer. Looking back I think Ms. Mackenzie was trying to tell me to hit the road but she was uncomfortable saying so. I can't blame her for that, I suppose. I could always set up another meeting with her and put the question to her again, but I had my answer.

The sounds coming from that room were like a world war two air raid siren telling me to make tracks. Momma made her bed and she was lying in it. Well, doing more than that actually.

I pulled Norma Jean from under my pillow and caressed her. She was good and sharp now—like a brand new blade. I've always got small carving projects scattered about my room. I grabbed one from my bedside table, flicked on my table lamp, and went at the carving. I had to be careful because I was carving on my back with a seriously sharp blade. I was making one of my many tiny totem poles. I'm obsessed with totem poles. I'm convinced I was an American Indian in another life. Maybe I'll do a twenty-three and me someday.

The moaning and groaning hit a crescendo, then stopped. Momma's bedroom door opened. My heart rate elevated slightly, as it always does. I killed my light. Footsteps drew close to my door and stopped. I gulped two lung-fulls of air. Silence. I fixed Norma in my hand. Readied her for an upward strike either under the chin or between the ribs. Half a minute seemed to take an hour to crawl by. The creak of the floorboard. Finally, the bathroom door down the hall opened and shut.

I emptied my lungs at the sound of running water. The toilet flushed, followed immediately by the door opening and closing. I leaped out of bed and stood to the side of the door. If he came in, my blade would dive into the side of his neck. Justifiable homicide. Sheriff Boulder and Deputy Tawanna would back me all the way. Hell, the town of Bucksville would be in my corner. An innocent high school girl full of hopes and dreams fights off the would-be rapist; any jury would let me walk. Heavy footfalls moved back to Momma's room. I relaxed. I shook out my cramping hand.

"The pig didn't even wash his hands," I said to myself as I wiped my sweaty palm on my t-shirt. I climbed back into bed, far too keyed up to sleep. On went the light and the carving back in my hands. As I worked the piece, a random thought bounced into my brain. The toilet seat would be left up and a good portion of piss would decorate the floor where a drunk missed the toilet. Tomorrow I'd fight with Momma about the mess until I'd eventually be the one to clean it up.

Shavings from my piece fell to the comforter. I blew them off and waited, pathetically, I might add, for the awful sounds from Momma's room to return. Happily, they did not. They must have passed out, thank god. It's the small victories that must be celebrated.

Really? Yeah, fuck that.

* * *

I got up early the next morning. Saturday, my favorite day of the week. I popped my bedroom window and checked the temperature. As expected, there was a chill in the air. By late morning it would warm up. I pulled on my mid-rise Stevie Flair Lucky jeans. I slipped on a pair of pink sockets and slid my feet into my favorite boots of all time: my stone-tumbled desert brush, motorcycle boots. They feel like a sneaker but are tougher than a workbook. I snapped on a black bra and pulled a black tank over it. Over this, I put on a two-toned blue checked, wool button-up, long sleeve. The hair went into a pony, which I pulled a backward ball cap over. With Norma on my hip and a folding knife in my pocket I put my ear to the door.

No human sounds. Good. I hustled to the bathroom, brushed my teeth, and did a quick wash of the face. I wanted to get the hell out of that shitty shack before the sex-birds got up.

The milk container was two days past spoiling and held barely enough for a quick bowl of cereal.

Thanks a lot, Momma.

I freed Norma from the scabbard and tossed the knife a hundred times; fifty right hand and fifty left hand. Satisfied, I popped earbuds in and hiked the trail behind my house. I sneer at the two-tone gray and black Chevy Silverado parked at an angle near our house. Momma's guest's truck. *Yuk.*

The trail continued on for about a twenty-minute easy hike to Raleigh Creek. The birds were out in full force, singing and chatting. Up overhead, a red-shouldered hawk circled. His circle seemed to ease to the west, which was the direction I was headed. It was nice to have an escort. I stopped a few times for quick tosses of Norma or my folding Buck at dead tree trunks. Only the dead ones.

Twenty minutes later, I was upon the creek. A big smile spread over my face when I saw who was at the creek with his fishing pole bobbing up and down in his hand. I've always been a big fan of Sheriff Jim Boulder. In fact, I'd bet he doesn't have an enemy from here to Los Angeles—same thing from here to Oregon. He threatens to retire every year, but we town-folk simply won't let him. There are a handful of other guys in town that might be up for the job, but they keep quiet about it, and Jim runs unopposed every election.

Half the girls in my senior class have crushes on him, which is why they make the same assumption about me. Obviously, that's not the case but I rarely deny it. Sometimes its just better to play along with the herd rather than upset it. I won't have anybody claiming that I doth protest too much. Screw that.

"G' morning, Sheriff. Catch anything?"

"Hey, Chloe," Sheriff Jim Boulder said, turning to face me. He smiled but then immediately turned away.

"Uh-uh I don't think so, Sheriff. Look at me. Sheriff, I've got Norma Jean with me. Show me that mug of yours, come on now."

He turned sheepishly.

"Who gave you that?" I asked, referring to his black and blue left eye.

"Not anyone from around here, I can tell ya that," he said. Jim was a big man. He wore a thick denim shirt and dark jeans. His back seemed to spread from the river to the county line. Whoever took a poke at the sheriff was either also a big man or liquored up to the point of mental instability.

"Oh, hang on, the light bulb just came on. It was the payday yesterday, wasn't it? What a drag for you, Sheriff. Are you and the deputies all right?"

"Oh sure, we made out all right. Feller did this is in the cooler, sleeping it off. I'll put the fear into him when he sobers up. By the way," he said, reeling in his line, "I told you about walking around with that weapon of yours. It's beyond the legal length."

"You did?" I said, my voice thick with playing dumb. We often went around like this. He didn't really mean it. "Sheriff, this is wild country. What if I'm attacked by a cougar?"

"Lot o' good that knife will do you." There was a slight chuckle in his voice.

I stopped a moment like I often do and sat on a rock beside the sheriff. I liked Sheriff Boulder. He was like a big brother and dad all in one. Decent and fair.

"Was it the boys out at the Miller Construction outfit?" I asked.

"It was indeed." He pulled on his line, then let it go slack.

"Why don't you guys call in law enforcement from other counties when it's payday. Y'all could use the help."

"Could we now? Maybe you want to bring that up at the next town hall."

"Don't be a smart ass, Sheriff," I said, nudging his shoulder for emphasis.

His laugh lines pronounced as a half-grin spread to his face. "Then don't tell me how to run my department."

I put my hands up in surrender. "I suppose some men like gettin' eye poked. My bad, Sheriff."

He turned and put his chestnut browns on me. He wasn't angry, but the smile was gone.

"Too far?"

"Nah, not really." He chuckled.

We sat and enjoyed the quiet for good fifteen minutes. It was comforting. Some couples married thirty years can't stand five minutes of quiet together. Now before you go thinking the mean girls are correct and that I've got a thing for the sheriff, check yourself. Sheriff Boulder is a good man. I like good men—good people, I should say. In case you missed it, the men in my life are a handful of teachers I don't respect and the men-children Momma drags into my world. Boulder is simply a breath of fresh air. I admire him the same way I do that red-shouldered raptor that accompanied me on my walk.

After the shared serenity, we eased into our usual small talk. Momma rarely came up. The sheriff and her had some kind of thing in the past, but I don't think it was romantic. But even if it was, I don't know if I'd care much. I know for a fact that he helped Momma and me when Daddy left. I'm also aware that it was a dark time for a lot of people in o'l Bucksville back then. As it stands, I'm good with leaving the past where she lies. Once the sheriff and I finished with the pleasantries, we went back to silence.

After about ten minutes, I said, "Creek bed's sure low."

"Yup."

I sat another five minutes, then stood and stretched my legs. "Well, Sheriff, it's clear to me you still don't know how to fish, so I'm going to shove along."

"You've got no patience kid. None of you millennials do." He smiled. "Besides, you should have seen the one that got away."

"See ya 'round, Sheriff," I said. "By the way, I'm Generation Z, not a millennial."

"There supposed to be some kinda difference?"

"Couple a years, yeah," I said. "And we're way cooler than those pussies." I leaned toward him and punched him on the shoulder. "And no more patty cake with the drunks, ya hear?"

"It ain't wise to strike an officer, Chloe," he said with his back to me.

"I'll be seein' ya, Sheriff."

Chapter Five

I savor my Saturday hikes. I often pull out the earbuds so that I can enjoy the songbirds as they share their verses and choruses. I wasn't ninety seconds down the trail when I heard the rumble of a vehicle engine. It was moving down the dirt road toward Raleigh Creek—where Sheriff Boulder was fishing. The engine had a deep rumble but it wasn't a truck, in which case I'd have kept on going. It was more like a Hemi or big block on a classic muscle car. That was probably why nosy Chloe stopped her trek and doubled back for a look.

I worked my way to a suitable clump of azalea shrubbery and crouched down low. A black late-model Chrysler 300 with blacked-out windows cruised down the road. The car listed and bobbed with each pothole. The sheriff looked over his shoulder briefly then went back to fishing. Or so it seemed. What I saw and what the driver would not have seen is that the sheriff reached to his hip and unsnapped the leather holster to his service weapon. Automatically and instinctively, I unsnapped Norma Jean's sheath. The vehicle came to a stop. A low trail of dust floated past the car. The car had one of those flat matte paint jobs. The only chrome left on the vehicle were the four H.E.M.I. letters.

Four doors opened. Four men got out. I knew exactly how the sheriff must have felt because I felt the same way. The question was simple: what the hell do these assholes want? I wouldn't have wanted to be in Boulder's position. With the river in front of him he was essentially pinned down. These guys clearly weren't tourists searching for a pristine picnic spot. Or a family of four that happened down the wrong road. They sought out Boulder, and they found him. I stroked Norma Jean at the hilt.

The man at the front of the pack had the actor Josh Brolin's good looks. He stepped forward. He wore black loafers, black dress pants, and a tight black t-shirt to match. His cobalt blue blazer was unbuttoned and was clearly tailor-made. It was, no duh, he was the leader. Black Raybans shielded his eyes from the sun. He used both hands to move his thick black hair back from his forehead. He stroked twice with both hands, then three times with a single hand.

What the fuck is that supposed to signify?

"Sheriff Boulder, how're the fish bitin'?"

He knew the sheriff but the sheriff didn't know him. Classic intimidation tactic. Boulder casually put his rig down and faced the four visitors. He ignored the phony friendly intro.

"What can I do for you, fellas?" Boulder asked.

The sheriff had the water to his back—not good. My guess was the leader had something at the small of his back, maybe a Glock or beretta. Boulder's Glock was on his hip. Henchman number one, who looked mixed native and white and sported the same blazer, however off the rack, probably packed as well. The biggest guy was every bit the dimensions of Boulder maybe fifteen pounds north of him, which would top him out at around two-hundred and sixty pounds. He would be the slowest on the draw if he was strapped. That left the guy I'd call the quiet one even though, so far, the leader was the only one to speak. Quiet One's movements seemed soundless. And it was if his eyes were quiet, if that's actually a thing. He was probably the scariest of the group. His orange-brown eyes were focused, pained, and held a little bit of sadistic intent behind them. I'm sure he gave Boulder the most concern.

And then there was me and Norma Jean. I had no desire to get near this mess. I had every confidence the sheriff would reason his way out of the jam. Because no way, good as he is, could the sheriff drop four men off the draw. That's Hollywood bullshit.

Fuck. Shit. Fuck.

I asked myself how far I'd go to help the sheriff, armed with only two knives. Then I told myself to shut the hell up and stay focused. The notion was paralyzing to think about.

"Right to the point, okay then. We've got a little business in these parts, and we're hoping it's not going to be a problem."

"Stay on the right side of the law, and it won't be." Boulder kept his hands at his sides. Non threatening, but ready…and we all knew it.

"Oh, we're law abiding, Sheriff, I assure you."

The ring leader smiled the entire time he spoke. Problem was it was the type of smile that sat there during a gentle moment, but would also sit there if he were kicking puppies. He looked as if torture was his thing.

"Thing is, Boulder—"

"Sheriff Boulder," Jim Boulder said. His voice carried the authority it no doubt had back when he was a Highway Patrol officer. 'Step out with your hands up' sort of authority.

"Sheriff. Thing is, I happen to know that small towns like Bucksville have laws, yes, but they also have their kinda redneck way o' doing things."

I wasn't close enough to see it but I know Sheriff Boulder, and I knew in that moment his jaw muscles were flexing and contracting with rage. He hated these assholes every bit as much as I did. More even since he was a man with a badge.

I tend to watch movies with Marilyn Monroe, hence the name of my knife. But in that moment, I wish we were in a western film where the good sheriff put the assholes down for good.

"I don't know what your business is or what your game is and frankly I don't give a damn. You don't back a lawman against a body o' water without sayin' something." He kept his eyes on the leader the entire time, but I'm sure he scanned all four men in his periphery.

"Now get back in your vehicle and move it along before I call in my deputies."

Deputies! What a moron. Why didn't I think of that? Damn it, Chloe. I pulled out my cell phone and texted Deputy Bad Ass. Her name is actually Raven Tawanna, and she is one tough Chickasaw woman. Students at my school, including the boys, are terrified of her. Not me. I want to be that bitch when I grow up. I'd never refer to her as the B-word, mind you. If she were side by side with Boulder, I'd bet all my savings on the two of them walking out of that showdown without a scratch.

I fired off a text, not wanting to risk being heard by the assholes. I hoped she wasn't far, because if anything happened to the sheriff, it would be on me. I should have called in the cavalry moons ago.

Nice use of the 4.0 GPA dumbass!

Boulder's posture told me he was done talking. The crew either had to make a move or hop in the Hemi and back the hell out of there. The ring leader took three steps toward the sheriff.

"That's far enough," Boulder said. He moved his hand to his holster and remember, he was already unstrapped.

"Whoa, whoa," the leader said. He pulled off his sunglasses and held his hands away from his body. Even with the tension thicker than molasses, the puppy-kicking smile sat pasted to his face.

He told his guys to take it easy, then backed up slowly. "Okay, Sheriff, we'll let you get back to your fishing." He said. "We really just stopped by as a courtesy."

None of the men took their eyes off the sheriff until they got in the car. It powered up and then reversed slowly up the dirt road. Again, bobbing and juking, pushing the shocks to the limit.

Once it was out of sight, Boulder barked, "Get the hell out here, Chloe!"

I walked like a toddler who'd done a lot more than spill the milk.

"Is this a game to you? Do you get off on this kinda crap? I know your life's tough but this is no joke. What if they saw you?"

"I'm sorry. Look," I said and held up my phone as if it were Exhibit A in a court of law. "I texted Deputy Tawanna. Clearly, you needed back up."

"I don't give a god damn—these guys are—"

He turned toward the creek and let loose another 'god damn it.' He spun around and closed the distance between us fast. He towered over me. A massive index in my face froze me in place.

"These guys are looking for trouble. They see you, they cap me, and guess who's next on their menu of—god damn it, Chloe!"

His face grew red. His neck muscles bulged with veins pulsating. I wasn't afraid, but boy, was I ashamed. One minute we're friends, the next, he's my dad giving me shit. My bottom lip began to quiver. The water behind my eyeballs built and threatened to leak.

Nuh-uh, Screw that!

Right or wrong, I'm not good with men barking at me. I sucked in a deep breath of air. I thrust my own finger at him.

"Don't fucking yell at me, Sheriff. I told you I called Raven and," I paused, "here she comes now. You're welcome!"

Deputy Raven Tawanna came in fast without sirens. The Ford Explorer S.U.V. skidded to a stop. Tawanna's police-issue boots slammed onto the dirt. Her hair was back in a ponytail. She wore faded blue jeans, which Boulder allowed, the pale blue Bucksville deputy button-up, and her sheriff's jacket. She looked to her boss first.

"Assholes in the 300 I passed?"

Boulder nodded. Raven Tawanna put her eyes on me but didn't say anything. Her body was neither taught nor relaxed, just ready. Her silence had electricity to it. My original plan was to bale after my fit with Boulder but when Deputy Bad Ass showed up I felt as though I should wait to be dismissed. I can be a hard ass, but in the presence of Tawanna, I'm a newborn lamb separated from the flock. I'd bet a full two minutes passed before the deputy spoke.

"What are you two fighting about?" she said finally.

Boulder and I looked at each other sheepishly. Neither of us was surprised Raven picked up on our vibe. In fact, the two minutes of silence was probably her way of letting us cool off. It worked. I was able to put together that Boulder got hot with me because he was scared for me. And I, well, as I said, I don't do men shouting at me. Or crossing me in any way, for that matter. I still felt like an idiot for not calling Raven earlier.

With the dust-up settled, Boulder and I took turns bringing the deputy up to speed. She didn't say anything, nor did she have questions for us. No surprise there. She simply downloaded our tale and did whatever it is she does with information.

"I'm going into town and keep an eye on them," she said and walked to her vehicle.

"I'll run the plate. Meet you in the office later," Sheriff Boulder said.

We watched Tawanna gun it in reverse up the narrow road. Boulder and I looked at each other and nodded in unison. He stalked toward his S.U.V., and I moved off down the trail.

Chapter Six

Normally I enjoy the walk home. In addition to the songbirds, I practically imbibe nature's plethora of scents. Lavender, jasmine, sage, evening primrose, and more flood the nostrils with each step. But after that episode, I couldn't shake the douchebags in the Chrysler 300 from my mind. Not to mention my screw up calling Raven so late. You'll notice it's not the first time I'm chastising myself about the late call. Nobody's harder on Chloe than Chloe. That's a quote from my guidance counselor. I took it as a compliment. The minute I ease off the gas on myself is the minute I'm losing. And I hate losing.

When I trekked the last portion of the trail my heart sunk when I saw Momma's 'guest' Chevy Silverado still parked near the bottom step. The screen door was closed but the front door was open.

Shit, they're up.

In a semi-unconscious move, my hand brushed my hip searching for the sense of security Norma Jean gave me. Anxiety hammered at my heart like a battle ax. I fought to keep it under control as I vaulted the steps. I hauled the screen door open and saw a big frame, a man's frame, in front of the fridge. *My* fucking fridge. I couldn't make out his features due to having moved from the bright sunshine to the dark indoors.

"Well, good morning. Who might you be?" His voice was deep but sounded put-on.

"Who *might* I be?" I said. That was all I was giving him. I didn't like the way he asked his stupid question.

"Yo, Joselyn there's a pretty young thing out here. Kinda favors you," the man called. The smell of booze on him seemed fresh—this morning's pull, not last night's party.

"You got a name?"

"Chloe," I said. He caught the fury in my eyes and stood aside from the fridge. I hauled the door open and took inventory. It was as I suspected: Momma contributed nothing, and she and her new friend were already into the beer.

Momma came out in a robe with a towel around her head. She pulled the towel off and shook out her wet hair.

"I see you two have met," Momma said. Although I hadn't actually gotten the big goof's name.

"Name's Brett," he said through the gap in his front teeth. He offered me a hand. I didn't so much as look at it, let alone take it.

"Pleasure's mine," I said and walked to my room.

"Don't be rude, Chloe, we've got company," Momma said. As if any of her 'friends' ever warranted courtesy.

"Didn't I say the pleasure was mine?" I called over my shoulder before closing my door behind me. I pulled Norma out and checked her. I'm not sure why and thought maybe it was like how cops and cowboys check their guns for rounds in the middle of shoot-outs. I grabbed my keys and opened the door to leave.

"Why wouldn't you shake my hand? I was just being friendly."

His grin said exactly what he wanted...and it wasn't Momma. He was about thirty, which put him at least fifteen years past the age he should be to have as much acne as he did. He was almost as big as Sheriff Boulder, but it was his eyes I didn't like. They were mean to the point of cruel. I never knew how Momma picked 'em and I didn't want to know. I just needed to get the hell out of there. But now, this idiot blocked my exit.

"How long you staying?" I asked because if he was leaving that day, I'd stock the fridge. If not, they could buy their own shit, and I'd stash my food in my bedroom mini-fridge.

Fuck my life!

"Why, you want me to stay?" he said, slowly sliding a hand up the casing to

29

the top of the door frame. His hip jutted out to the side. He probably thought he looked like a Hollywood leading man.

Huh, far from it, asshole.

"I need you to move," I said. "Please."

"Take it easy, darlin'. I just want to know, again…" he paused. "Why you wouldn't…shake…my hand?"

I leaned in close and growl-whispered. "Listen fuck-stick, you can screw my mother all you want, but you can't touch me. Ever. Not even a fucking handshake, got it? Now move!"

I shoved him hard on the shoulder. He let me leave but it wasn't like my shove had the power to move his bull-like body. That's why I say he *let* me leave. I'd hate to be within a mile of him when he'd want it to go another way. Even with Norma Jean…

"Why can't you get along with people?" Momma asked as I headed for the door. I ignored her. My blood pressure and heartrate were way too high to get into it with her. I brought my Nissan Frontier truck to life and let her run a moment. My face was hot, and my armpits began to moisten with a combination of fear and anger-sweat.

This shit needs to end.

I eased the shifter into drive and rolled away toward town. I needed a Geraldine's breakfast and fast.

* * *

The door chimed as I entered Geraldine's Diner. As always Geraldine's smile made me smile—in spite of the mess that just happened. Her smile not only lit up a fifty-meter perimeter, but it also said she was happy to see you and wanted a hug. Her perfect dental work sparkled along with her eyes.

"Well, if it isn't my favorite person in the world," Geraldine said.

"Hey-hey Ger,"I said. "Boy, it smells amazing in here."

"Hey, I thought I was your favorite person," Dave Edmonds teased.

Dave was a long-haul trucker who carried a torch for Geraldine since they were kids. Geraldine's husband had been in the second tower during 9-11.

It was clear to everyone Geraldine would never love again. Dave knew it and seemed to accept his role as distant admirer. As the ever loyal Labrador retriever, he respected Geraldine's feelings. And although she loved Dave as a dear friend, she'd never love him or any man like she did her husband, Walter.

I moved toward an empty red leather counter stool. By the time I sat, Geraldine had already filled my cup with coffee and placed the silver tin creamer beside it. I like a hefty amount of cream and a touch of sugar. As I raised the cup to my mouth, her eyebrows came together in a frown, and the corners of her mouth dipped.

"Oh no, sweetheart, not again," she said.

"Is it that obvious?"

"Well, it is payday weekend, and I know your mother," she said with a sigh. "I mean no offense, sweetheart."

"No offense taken, Geraldine. I don't think you'd be capable of offending even if you knew how."

"Ha!" She blurted and rocked her head back. "Darlin', if I was a celebrity, I'd hire you as my publicist. I kid you not."

She stepped back with a hand on her hip and the coffee pot in the other. "Now, you stay put, I need to top up some cups then I'll be right back," she said. "Will you be having the regular?"

I gave her a weak 'yes' grin.

As she walked away, she called out my entire order over her shoulder as she did with all the regulars. "Chet, three eggs done easy, hash browns, Geraldine's biscuit with sweet honey-butter on the side…and bacon." She turned and winked. "Three strips."

"I'm on it, Ms. G," Stan, the cook, replied.

I got a few glances from patrons. More than likely because it probably seemed like a lot of food for someone my size. Again, I'm not petite, but I'm curvy small. It didn't bother me, though—it'd be silly for them to judge when we're all eating from the same trough, more or less. Especially when most of them were carrying more than a little extra real estate around their middle areas…if you catch my implication.

Chapter Seven

I was nearly finished my meal when the door chimed. I didn't have to check who entered. The other diners pipped up plenty when Sheriff Boulder walked in. That was pretty much custom. The man was loved. He greeted everyone with hellos and head nods before stepping to the breakfast bar. But he didn't take a seat. He put his foot on the six-inch high brass foot-ledge and removed his Stetson.

"Morning, Ger. You got a minute?"

Geraldine said she did and moved opposite the sheriff and leaned forward on her plump elbows. They did their best to keep voices low but I've got the hearing of a fruit bat—plus I'm kinda nosy like that.

The sheriff gave Geraldine an abridged version of his visit from the outsiders while fishing. I was glad of my fly on the wall position because I had some context. And what I saw in the sheriff was unsettling. He was agitated, and he doesn't rattle easily or often. Eventually, he got around to asking Geraldine if she'd seen the fellows.

"They came in but just stayed for coffee," Geraldine said.

The sheriff scratched his chin, "Anything else?"

"They made their way onto the boardwalk and strutted like they could buy the town of Bucksville at the drop of a hat."

"Yeah, well, you let me know if you hear or see anything else."

"See something, say something. I know the drill sheriff."

"Thanks, Ger"

"Anytime, Sheriff."

The sheriff backed off the counter and placed his hat back on his head. A chorus of goodbyes followed him out the door. I rushed to finish my meal. I had work to do.

I paid up and left a hefty thirty-five percent tip, which Geraldine refused to take at first.

"Must we always do this, Ger? Come on, it's rude to deny someone who's trying to do something nice."

She couldn't argue that one.

"All right, sweetheart, but your next breakfast is on me."

"Now, how does that make any sense, Ger? Just stop."

She let out a big sigh, came around the counter, and squeezed me like a bear.

"You be safe out there now, ya hear?"

"Always," I said. "Say, what about these outsiders riling up the sheriff?"

"You heard every word, nosy-nosington, so don't ask me nothin', Geraldine said, raising an eyebrow.

"I can't imagine for one second the sheriff wants you sticking your nose in, regardless o' how close you two are," she said. She used the end of a pen to scratch a portion of her head, which was done up in a bee hive.

"Matter o' fact, that's all the more reason to stay out of his business."

She moved back behind the counter as a message that the conversation was closed. I didn't bother mentioning that I was at the scene when the Chrysler pulled up. It would only catch me more grief. I thought I'd sit on it for a while.

"Just a concerned citizen is all," I said.

Geraldine peered over the rim of her glasses, "Mm hmm. Just keep your head in them books, stay out of the sheriff's affairs, and keep Norma Jean handy."

I stroked Norma at my hip. "I can do at least two of those things, Geraldine."

She snapped her counter rag at me. "Go on git girl. I got a business to run."

* * *

Main Street bustled with Saturday traffic. Most of the townsfolk shopped on Saturdays. Pushing close to noon, some of the out of town construction workers began showing their hungover faces. They'd hit Geraldine's, Chollys, or one of the taco joints. Then in an hour from now, they'd be back on bar stools riding the booze train express. Some would go all day while others would take an afternoon nap, like an Italian pisolino, before emerging at night to fill up the bars. I didn't envy the sheriff and his deputies.

I crossed Main Street. A red and white classic Ford Bronco stopped for me. I gave a thank-you wave. Everybody J-walks in Bucksville. I imagine the same goes for most small towns. I stepped up onto the wooden boardwalk, which is a touch the city installed for the tourists at the end of last year. The idea being that tourists will get the feeling they've stepped into an old gold rush town. One hundred and ten percent cornball cheesy, but what do I know?

As my boots clipped and clopped down the planks, I noticed Sheriff Boulder inside the hardware store jawing it up with Simon, the owner. My plan was to get groceries at the Green Grocer and load up my mini-fridge. I knew in my gut Momma's new 'friend' would probably hang out for the whole weekend. Seeing the sheriff with Simon reorganized my plan. I needed in on that conversation.

As I was about to cross, someone off to my left pumped the accelerator two times. Whatever was under the hood had some significant horsepower to it. Cat calls followed the engine's rev. I didn't turn, but I did peer out of the corner of my eye. The revs and calls were for me. It was a Chrysler 300, all flat matte, tinted windows, and ridiculous rims. I didn't need a 4.0 grade point average to know this was the crew that paid Jim Boulder a visit. I'd have chalked them up to being standard losers and moved on, but they rattled Boulder and I didn't like it. And then short-fuse-Chloe showed up.

"Go play with yourselves, ya dickless wonders," I shouted, spinning toward the vehicle. The car screeched to a halt. Henchman, number one, the mixed raced indigenous looking guy leaned a thick arm out the window.

"What the hell did you say, girlie?" he said.

"Girlie? What is this, the 1940s? Get the fu—"

"Hey," he said and pointed a thick finger at me. "Show some respect, or I'll teach you some manners. Won't I, boss?" he said and turned his head toward the driver.

I could have hit the man between the brows with Norma Jean, and she'd enjoy it—we both would.

Calm down, Chloe.

A tourist family, mom, dad, and twin boys about six years old stopped and watched the spectacle. It appeared as though our little display was ruining their vacation. The mother clutched her boys close. To the husband's credit, he stepped up.

"Leave the girl alone, why don't ya, fellas?"

"Mind your business less you want a beating in front of your kids," the henchman said.

The Chrysler rev'd twice and rolled down Main Street. The husband and wife team shook their heads.

"Thank you, sir, you didn't have to do that," I said.

"Oh, you're very welcome," he smiled.

"Oh, and sorry about the language in front of your kids. My bad."

"Not at all," he said with a wave of his hand. His wife, clearly over the ordeal, gave me a sideways look. In her mind, I went from victim to threat to her marriage in under two minutes flat.

Get over yourself, lady.

Chapter Eight

Both men's heads turned as I entered. The sheriff had already removed his hat and held it in one hand at his side.

"Afternoon, Sheriff," I said. " Simon," I added.

Simon's grin was welcoming. He had the type of smile that appeared as though he was on the brink of laughter, and would bust up just as soon as he let you in on the joke. The sheriff on the other hand held his mouth in a flat line and narrowed his eyes. A moment later, he softened a touch. He knew I was stalking him. We know each other that well.

"What brings you in today, Chloe? Another project on the home?"

"Happily no, Simon. The place is holding up pretty good for now," I said. "I'm actually here—"

"No, Chloe," the sheriff said. Simon wore a look of confusion.

"I'm here to join this conversation."

"Oh?" Simon said.

The sheriff swiveled his large frame to face me.

"This is serious stuff here, Chloe, I told you that."

"Sheriff, I can help. From the sidelines, I mean."

"Dang it, Chloe, you're like a Pitbull terrier with a chew toy. This is police business. I don't want you sticking your nose in."

Simon brought out a pair of silver pliers and began rubbing them with a rag like a bartender would polish a rocks glass.

"You ever have success talking a woman out of something she's got an interest in, Sheriff?" Simon paused. "And Chloe's about the most stubborn gal in Bucksville."

I took the comment as a compliment. The sheriff breathed out heavily.

"All right, you can be privy to this conversation, being that this is public space and all, but you're not a part of this in any way, ya hear?"

"I hear...sir." It was all I could do to contain a nervous giggle building inside.

A space of quiet passed through. Simon polished. The sheriff chose words, and I waited impatiently, leaning against the counter with arms folded.

"You were saying, Simon," the sheriff said.

"Well, they come in here and split up. An old shoplifter's trick, but I've got six mirrors and I only need two eyes to watch 'em both. Didn't take long for me to realize they weren't here to rob me. It seemed intimidation was the desired goal. Can't say why other than muscle flexin'. Which, if that was the case, it was intended for each other—kind of pecking order, chest-puffing nonsense. Cause I wasn't rattled one bit."

Boulder did that thing he does when he's pissed and tries not to show it. His jaw muscles contract and relax. Added air in his lungs made his barrel chest expand. And his eyes—his eyes turned mid-December frosty.

"My guess is the crew hasn't been a unit for very long. This would be why each one wants to show his peacock feathers," he paused and put the pliers down. "Just my guess, though."

"I thought the same thing," I blurted. "Sorry. I thought the same thing when I saw them out at the creek. The quiet one worried me a little, though. What did you think, Sheriff?"

The sheriff's look would have made a cage fighter piss himself. To say I regretted my outburst is an understatement. Simon came to my rescue.

"You mean the one with the light brown eyes of an orange tabby cat? Yes, he could give a damn about posturing and flexing. Difficult to know his agenda, however. A lot behind the eyes—not much of it good."

The sheriff scratched his chin, considering Simon's words. The shopkeeper picked up a different set of pliers and took the rag to it. I've known Simon a long time. Menial tasks help him focus his thoughts. It's also part of his love of holding court. Polishing his wrenches add to the theatrics. It's similar to me sharpening my blades. It helps me think, but there are no theatrics with me.

"Anyway," he continued. "They wandered up and down the aisles picking up items here and yon. The leader is a greaseball of a fella with a leading man's square cut jaw. He's got the confidence of a mountain lion only in the body of a deer fawn. And enough fancy cologne to choke a healthy horse." He said, waving the rag in front of his face. As if the memory itself was pungently palpable. He continued on with the one-man play.

"It appears you're on the top of his dance card, Jim. He asked darn near twenty questions about you."

The sheriff picked up a pack of carpenter's pencils and turned it over in his hand. He gave Simon a moment in case there was more.

"What did you give them—info wise?"

"As you know, Jim, I can say a whole lot o' nothing with an abundance of words, most of which make sense." He laughed. "Until the other party grows weary and takes their questions elsewhere."

Jim stared into his hat a moment before putting it back on. "True, I've been on the receiving end of more than a few of your ramblings. You've led me so deep into the woods I needed a compass to get back."

Simon shot me a grin like he'd just been named valedictorian.

"I appreciate it, Simon. I expect they intend to hang around a bit before making their 'bad intention' known." The sheriff tipped his hat, moved to the door, and stopped.

"I just had a run-in with them, Sheriff," I said. I think they forgot I was there, which was fine with me. Both men had eyebrows raised so I told them of my street episode. Anger flooded back into Boulder's eyes. Simon's emotions read anger, sympathy, and concern.

"All right," the sheriff said. "Everybody stay sharp. See something, say something. And Chloe—"

He didn't bother with the warning all three of us knew was coming. With the door opened, he asked Simon a final question.

"Did these fellas actually buy anything?"

"Do you mean axes, knives, sledgehammers, and a whole wack of fertilizer for bomb making? I'd have volunteered that if they had."

"Yup, I suppose you would have. Thanks for your time, Simon. Chloe." He tipped his hat before closing the door behind him.

Chapter Nine

I didn't buy a whole lot at the Green Grocer, just two days' worth of grub: chicken and fish, some vegetables, snacks, coffee, cream, and a few toiletries. I moved quickly through the aisles. It isn't easy moving fast through a grocery store on a Saturday in a small town. You can't simply brush off all the friendly people dying to catch up with you—even if nothing has changed since the last ten times you saw them.

Still, politeness is best because rudeness kills. Because once you get the scarlet letter 'B' for bitch tattooed on you in a town like Bucksville, it's tough to get along. Kyle, the checkout boy is in my physics class. As he helped bag my groceries he asked if I was going to the bonfire party that night.

"Nah, Kyle, those things aren't for me."

"Aw, come on, Chloe, ya gotta let your hair down once in a while."

"I gotta look after Momma tonight," I said. I grabbed my bag and hoisted it on my shoulder.

"I heard she met someone so…" he hesitated and shifted foot to foot.

"So what?"

"*So* she'll be busy hanging out with the dude, *so* you should hang out with us."

"Look, Kyle, no, sorry, I can't. I can't be around drunk high school seniors when I have the luxury of being around my drunk mother." My tone carried equal parts venom and sarcasm.

"Ouch."

"You're right, that was bitchy, sorry."

"No, no, I get it. It was a dumb thing to invite you to."

"You didn't invite me, Kyle. You asked if I was going?"

His cheeks rouged up. "Huh? Okay, wait I—"

"Ya gotta be prepared, my man." I punched him lightly on the shoulder, then booked. He looked like a game show contestant that went with option B instead of option A, when in his gut he was leaning toward A all the time.

* * *

This time when I saw Momma's latest indulgence's pickup truck parked in front of our place I was more pissed than anxious. Pissed is better, believe me. I can't say I was surprised, but I'd be lying if I said I wasn't hopeful the bastard had moved on. I walked in, mumbled hello, and took the groceries to my room. A combination of boredom and Sheriff Boulder's problem chewing at me had me log into Instagram. Three minutes later, I logged off. The lovebirds ignored me as I went outside to tend to my knife throws.

I was surgical even while on automatic pilot. But I suppose that's the goal, right? Muscle memory? I needed to know why these assholes with a hard-on for Boulder were in town. What was their end game? Toss after toss, the droning 'thunk' sound of Norma sinking into poplar wood became soothing. By the time I was done, I'd actually worked up a bit of a sweat. I went back inside and straight to my room. Momma and dipshit were drunk dancing and laughing in the living room. Clearly, pain was not felt by either party.

Get a life, assholes.

I grabbed one of my folding knives and sliced up some apples, cheese, and pepperoni. A handful of cashews and dried apricots rounded out my dinner. I opened up Youtube and watched mixed martial arts demonstrations while I worked a couple of carvings. With each demonstration, I picture using it on the drunkard in the next room. Purely in a self defense manner of course. At least that's how I'd tell it in court. Every so often, my thoughts drifted to Kyle. In a way, I was drawn to him with his thick hair, which is a gorgeous blend of styled meets messy. His eyes were playful even when he struggled to keep his flirtatious game together. Which, was fucking hot, by the way. There's something sexy about the hot, cool guy fighting to hang on to his cool.

But I always kept Kyle at arm's length. In part because too many chicks wanted him, but more because he didn't fit into my plans. I could just see myself heading to the airport, all set for my European adventure, then asking the Uber driver to turn around because I'd fallen for a boy. Annoying. I'd kill myself if I let myself get derailed like that.

And just like that, I realized I'd spaced out within the first two minutes of the Youtube video. I decided to continue carving in bed.

* * *

I'm a light sleeper, always have been. And there's no mystery as to why. I'd dozed off on top of my comforter and woke when I heard Momma and company take the party to the bedroom. It was always loud and passionate at the start. With fingers in ears, I headed to the bathroom and got ready for bed. I hurried my routine in case Romeo-Brett needed to piss before finishing his business with Momma…ugh. Back in bed with a pillow over my head, slumber took me at some point. Somewhere in the wee hours, my inner radar jolted me up. The clock read 3:30 am. Norma was in my hands before I fully recognized the sound that woke me was my doorknob rotating back and forth.

This was next level intrusion, and I wasn't going to wait in bed for it. I hopped out and hid on the far side of the door. Norma was in my grip. Four other knives were strategically placed, and I alone knew the whereabouts.

The door rattled. The fucker was trying to force his way in. Why wasn't Momma ever enough for these assholes? In addition to my cutlery, I had a 19" Easton Beast Speed aluminum bat wedged between my bed and the wall. A loud bang sounded as he must have hammered the door with his fist.

"Fuck!" he said as if all females on the premises should be his and that daughters' bedroom doors should never be locked. What a dick. He went at the handle again, more vigorously this time. Norma Jean was itching to go to work. She was going straight into the intruder's neck if he breached the door. That was the one thing I knew. My speech was already rehearsed.

I feared for my life, Officer.

"Brett? Brett, honey, where are you?" Momma called. Her voice was drenched with booze and sleep.

Brett punched the door a second time and uttered the F word again. His footsteps moved away from my door at a pace half the speed of my beating heart. My shoulders dropped. I hadn't realized I'd been holding my breath. I held my spot for god knows how long. Once I heard the sex symphony start up again I kissed Norma Jean and crawled back into bed.

Unbelievable.

Chapter Ten

I bolted upright. The clock read 6:45 a.m. The tendrils of a dream slid off me like water going down a drain. God, I hoped it was a dream. It involved Brett with his hands all over me, except he seemed to have dozens of pairs of hands. He groped and clawed at my body. Norma stabbed and stabbed but for every hand I severed, two more took its place.

I tossed the comforter off and cracked my door and peeked through the crevice. Someone was in the bathroom. I quickly dressed then grabbed my toothbrush and paste set I keep on my desk. I brushed hurriedly and filled my mouth with water from the Swell bottle I keep in my mini-fridge. With a mouth full of toothpaste and water and Norma on my hip, I stepped outside and spat over the rickety railing.

"Well, that's certainly attractive."

I looked up and saw my bestie Shayna sitting atop her horse J.T., which was short for Justin Timberlake. She'd had a crush on Timberlake since I can remember. J.T. was a mostly walnut colored Appaloosa with a white spotted rump, cheeks, and nose. Shayna wore a red and white checkered button up long sleeve, faded wranglers, and black riding boots. She held her reins as well as a second set of reins in her hands. Attached to the other end was Rusty, the Thoroughbred she claimed as bad tempered. Also, my good buddy. Rusty was a beige-rusty color with a dark black mane and a tiny triangular shaped white spot on his head between his eyes.

"Got time for a ride, babe?"

"You've always seemed to know what I needed, Shay," I said. I patted Rusty on his nose and slapped him a few times on the shoulder.

"Ready to kick up some dust, old buddy?" I said to the gorgeous animal. He snorted and bobbed his head up and down. "Hang on."

I ran back inside and grabbed my boots, and came back out. I left my runners on the step and climbed aboard Rusty.

"Let's see if you remember how to ride one of these." Shayna smiled. She clicked her teeth and spurred her horse down the trail. Rusty, being a retired race horse, took off after J.T. This, I was ready for. Rusty wasn't a big prize winner in his day, but he wasn't a loser either. The trail was narrow. Rusty wanted to pass, but there was no room. Shayna's cackle told me she knew what Rusty was going through.

"Steady buddy, we'll take them on the open terrain. Hold tight now, boy." I got low and leaned forward and at times had to duck the low hanging sycamore tree branches. A quarter-mile down the trail, and we were into a clearing.

"Okay, buddy, let's show J.T. what you've got. Hyaah! Punch!"

Rusty accelerated as if being shot out of a cannon. I hadn't ridden in a while but it was all still there. It was as if Rusty and I were one. I could feel the movement of his musculature and knew his moves before he made them. We pulled level with Shayna and J.T. We smiled at each other a moment before Rusty sprung ahead. J.T. never had a chance. Nearing the edge of the clearing I reined the beast in with a 'whoa'. He didn't resist. He knew we'd won—nothing left to prove.

Shayna caught up and rode level with us. Both horses and riders panted heavily. We brought the horses down to a walk.

"Dang girl, I sooooo needed that," I said. "Thank you."

"I thought you might," Shayna smiled. "It's also why J.T. and I let y'all win."

"Let us—girl, you're so full of it your blue eyes are turning brown. We owned your asses out here," I said, patting Rusty on the shoulder.

"Ha, Rusty's passed it, girl. J.T. could have cleaned his clock if I let him."

"Well, maybe he was burdened. You look like you've put on a few pounds, girl. Just sayin.'"

"You scandalous bitch. Gimme them reins, you can walk your ass back to town."

Went back and forth like that for another ten minutes. It felt like we'd been ported back to when we were ten years old. Her laugh always triggered mine, then she'd totally lose it.

"God, I've missed you Shay," I said. I had tears in my eyes from laughing but now wondered if the other kind were coming.

"Back atcha, sis. I don't have any regrets doing the homeschool thing," she said. "Other than attending school with you. I'd love to be in the same classes and do whatever it is y'all do. Eat together in the cafeteria, sit in the bleachers—all that."

"I don't do any of that shit, Shay. I'm kind of a loner," I said. "Not lonely, though, just a loner. You know, with Momma..."

I didn't finish my thought. Momma talk would spoil this beautiful day, and I wasn't going to do that. Without even discussing it we tethered our horses to the large live oak tree like we'd done for years when we were growing up. We sat side by side at the base and looked out over the valley. The only sound was the horses grazing. The warm breeze was soothing on the face. The field was ripe with fragrant lemon scented sweet verbena.

"Sorry, Chloe."

"For what?"

"For you and me. We fell off because of me, not my homeschooling, and you and I both know it." She picked a yellow dandelion flower and spun it in her hand as she spoke. I pulled Norma, grabbed a stick, and went at it, which is what I do when I'm nervous. I'm usually barely aware of it.

"When Momma turned to drink, I turned away from you. I was, I don't know, scared, I guess. And that was bullshit. I should have been there for you. I'm a horrible friend."

I heard her sniffle. I don't remember what the hell I was doing to the stick but suddenly, my cheeks were soaked with tears. I dropped Norma, turned, and hugged Shayna. We squeezed each other tight. I was hanging on for friendship, crying for the lost years, and crying for myself. Crying for the years of Momma's lecherous boyfriends who never give me peace. I felt helpless. I couldn't leave, and I couldn't stay. But right then, in my best friend's arms, I felt like I mattered—mattered to someone. Someone I loved.

We pulled apart and wiped our faces. "You always were such a crybaby," I said. And sure enough, we were laughing again. We sat for what must have been an hour and caught up on everything as well as reminisced on our greatest hits.

Finally, "So, I've met someone."

"Ooh, does he look like Justin Timberlake? The singer, not the horse," I said. "Or does he look like a horse?" I laughed.

"Ha ha shut up and listen." She turned a shade more serious. My thinking was she was dating someone her daddy didn't like. I was preparing my 'date whoever you want' speech when Shayna threw me like Rusty threw me when we were young.

"*She* doesn't look like Timberlake, the singer or horse."

"She? Oh, I didn't—she—nuh-uh—really? You're dating a girl?"

She nodded. Her expression pleaded that I'd be cool with it.

"Wow, I didn't see that coming," I said. "Is she hot? Like as hot as me?" I laughed.

"Oh she's snack, babe, Sss-nack" she said. "Sorry."

'Snack' is essentially our term for 'hot' only in this case, hotter than hot. I hugged her again because I couldn't think of anything to say. When we pulled away, she seemed relieved.

"Wait, you didn't think I'd have a problem with you being gay, did you?"

"Not really, but you never know, Chloe."

"So, when do I get to meet her?"

"Oh, ah, anytime, soon, I guess."

She hadn't thought about that part.

"I'm happy you found someone, Shayna."

"Thanks," she said, pulling a few strands of hair and tucking it behind her ear.

"And thank you for what you said about you and me…and Momma and all that. It means a lot to me."

"Okay, don't get me crying again, bitch."

"Don't get me going either then," I said. "I've got a question for you."

"Shoot."

"All those sleepovers when were young, did you ever make a move when I was asleep?"

"Girl, I did so many things to you, I swear to god. I thought you were pretending to be asleep all those times."

"What..the..fuck!"

Shayna fell over laughing. "You idiot, what do you think I am, a pervert? You're so gross. You've always been FAM."

Gen z term of endearment for family.

"I'm just playing," I said. "In fact, now I'm a little hurt you never made a play for me."

"Oh, because lesbians hit on every girl that moves," she said, shaking her head.

"No, but I'm hot," I teased.

"Hot yes," she said. "But not my type. You're in the friend zone, I'm afraid."

We got up and got ready to ride.

"Tell me, Shayna," I said, mounting Rusty. "When did you fall out of love with Justin Timberlake?"

"Never loved him. It was always a smokescreen."

"Shit, don't let J.T. hear you," I said, nodding to her horse. I led Rusty away from the tree.

"Do your parents know you're out?"

"Told them three years ago. They said they'd always known."

"No fireworks or Hallmark movie blowup?"

"Nope, it went smooth like butt*ah*."

"I'm glad. Who else knows other than—oh shit, I didn't even ask her name. Now I'm the horrible friend."

"Alexis, but she goes by Lexi." Her face seemed to take on more sunshine. She was truly gone for the girl.

"Good for you. But is she really hotter than me? Like really snack?"

"Yup, sorry, again." She got a mischievous look in her eye. A look that took me back to our childhood. "By the way, anytime you want to join our team, let me know. I've got a membership, so I can vouch for ya."

"Eew, shut up," I said. "And stop looking at me that way. Come on, Rusty, there's a dangerous lesbo in these parts," I said and spurred him on. Shayna trailed behind me, cackling relentlessly. It was a beautiful sound. A sound I'd deeply missed.

Chapter Eleven

Brett the loser's truck was still parked in the same spot. They hadn't left the house as far as I could tell. I was going to go in but realized there was no need for it, to do what I wanted to do. I thought back to the goodbye hug from Shayna. She squeezed so hard I thought she might crack one of my ribs. She was obviously relieved to get the news off her chest and clearly over the moon that I was happy for her. I think the biggest thing for both of us was that we'd once again become as close as we ever had been in the past. All thanks to a couple of gorgeous horses and beautiful scenery. Unfortunately, the rekindling didn't make my decision to leave this town after graduation any easier. I'd miss the heck out of that girl.

I climbed into my truck, pulled out my phone, and did a quick internet search on the plates belonging to the Chrysler 300. With a username, password, and ninety-nine dollars a year on *Find A* plate.com I had the info in five minutes. The vehicle belonged to a Jesse Arlo.

I first checked for outstanding tickets. If there was a warrant, I could tell Sheriff Boulder, and the problem would go away. I have no doubt he and his office would be ahead of me on this, but still, I wanted to know.

Arlo didn't have any outstanding warrants but he certainly had his fair share of traffic tickets in his past. No surprise there. Apparently, he had a penchant for depressing the accelerator when police were in the vicinity. The car is a heat score to begin with but on top of that, he's obviously too friggin' stupid to buy a radar detector. This made him dumb A.F.

A.F. is short for As Fuck in Generation Z speak. Just F.Y.I.

Next, I checked for any liens on the vehicle. There was one in 2013, but it was paid off by what appeared to be a previous owner. Nothing there on Arlo. I decided to scout around his socials, which would be the easiest task for me. It looked as though Jesse Arlo hadn't posted on Facebook in at least three years. That could mean he was legit up to three years ago, then, due to shifting to a life of crime, shut down his social media.

Maybe he got so busy he forget to wipe the Facebook account. Or maybe he tried to scrub the page and he got fed up with it. It's a real pain in the ass closing a Facebook account. Trust me. Been there.

Of the three other men in what I'll call the 300 crew, two of them ran with Arlo back in the early days. One was the thick-necked goon, and the other a skinny henchman, who in my opinion, is a total Jesse sycophant. There were several shots of the three mostly hanging around an auto body shop. Chop shop? If I were keeping notes I'd have highlighted chop shop and added a question mark in yellow. Jesse always wore street clothes. Not like his slick blazer, slacks, and loafer get-up but jeans, t-shirts, and sports jerseys. Primarily Dodgers gear.

The other two clowns were almost always in coveralls. Sometimes full-on, and other times the top half was tied at the waist revealing tatted arms and torsos covered by thin wife beaters.

Wife beater. How is that still a thing?

A ton of shots were taken in front of the business with the sign in plain sight: Arlo's Autobody Shop. I switched my search to the business and plugged in 'images.' A half dozen pictures sprung up. I clicked on the info tab off to the right. Arlo's Autobody Est. 2015 closed Feb. 2020. No explanation as to the closure. It could have been any number of reasons. Poor management. Jesse's criminal career took off. Maybe the business was an early victim of the COVID 19 economic breakdown. Too many possibilities.

I began to feel butterflies of excitement flutter in my belly. This would be good stuff to pass on to Boulder and officer Bad Ass. I was of two hemispheres. On one hand, I felt like the dutiful little citizen of Bucksville, while the other part of me was the annoying little nerd with no life and nothing better to do. Was I any different from nerdy online gamers?

Which head voice would I listen to? Screw it, helping out Bucksville's finest was the right thing to do. I told myself that was the angel's voice on my shoulder. I'd listen to her, not the guy with the pitchfork and horns.

I opened up Yelp and checked for customer reviews. Arlo's had plenty. Most were positive. But I was on the hunt for the negative reviews. There's no guarantee the reviews are accurate because some people just like to hate. Still, this chick needed to dig in and read between the lines if necessary. We covered crap like this in an entrepreneurial class I took as an elective when I was a junior. I crushed that course.

I stopped on a few photos along the way. It was no surprise there were a ton of muscle cars, both late model and classics. I really don't know much about chop shops, so I couldn't tell which cars were 'hot' or legit body jobs. I'd leave that stuff to the sheriff.

After finding the first negative review, my excitement grew. I speed read three others and found a common theme. To quote my favorite: *"These A-holes are shady A.F. Avoid at all cost."* I think they meant 'all costs' because originally, the phrase was "at any cost" then around 1910 or so, "at all costs" became the hip idiom. I told you I was nerdy…although I prefer the term*bookish bitch*. Whatever…

Another five minutes of that, and I'd had enough. After all, I wasn't trying to solve a case. I just wanted to add evidence to the pile. My belly butterflies continued to flutter.

* * *

I slid my phone into my inside jean jacket pocket. As I was about to turn the engine over Brett the loser came out onto the porch with a grin on his face, empty of any I.Q. points.

"Hey, you. Whatcha doin' out there in your truck?"

I leaned my head out the window. "Well, ya see, if you turn the key, it goes vroom- vroom and I get the hell outta here."

I punched the gas and spit dirt and gravel in my wake. When I checked my rearview, he was waving the dust away with his arm. It was a childish move on my part, but the guy made my spinal cord hurt. I could die an early death trying to understand why Momma does it. How she could let a man like that put hands on her, let alone…ew!

* * *

Sheriff Boulder's dirt driveway was a little over a quarter-mile long and ran straight from the road to his log home. If someone wanted to sneak up on the lawman, they'd have to come from either east or west through the woods. Halfway up the drive, I saw him sitting on his porch on a wooden chair made with thick round cedar tree stocks for armrests. Deputy Tawanna made it for him on his fortieth, and it was Boulder's favorite chair. I slowed the truck down so the dust wouldn't choke him out when I pulled up.

His thin lips were in a thin line that read contentment. His right cowboy boot rested on his left knee. A Rawlings, which is a locally brewed beer, sat on the two-by-six wood railing in front of him within reach. He allowed himself a half-smile as I came and rested my boot at the bottom step.

"I'm gonna use my policing skills that I've honed over the years and deduce that you've come with info," he said. "Or what you think is info, on our visitors. Yes?"

"I'll be really impressed if you tell me what I have before I say it."

"I'm not here to impress, Chloe," he said. "Except to impress upon you that you should stay out of police business."

"You just turned our fun banter into, well, un-fun."

He reached for the beer and killed it. "What can I do for you, young lady?" His sighing breath was exaggerated. He stood and walked inside. I took it as an invitation and followed him.

Boulder's home was practically a shrine to wood. In addition to the thick log walls and beams, most of the furniture was made from wood. It was as though he'd walked into a thick stand of trees and carved his home straight from the forest. Naturally, this was another area where the sheriff and I bonded. He even had a few totem poles I'd carved for him over the years sitting on various shelves and the fireplace mantel. I was a little embarrassed at the pride I felt at seeing my work in the private man's home. He returned from the kitchen with a beer for himself and headed toward one of two Morris chairs, which sat at an angle to one another. A small chunky wood end table sat between the chairs. The dark leather cushion wheezed as he sat. He knew better than to offer me a beer—I was not insulted.

"Spill," he said.

"I checked out the Chrysler 300's plate," I said, holding up a piece of paper.

"We did the same, Chloe, we're law enforcement, remember?" His voice ticked up a half decibel point. I never like to rile the sheriff up, but at the same time, I am the way I am—dogged, badgerly, mule-stubborn, take your pick. I knew I had a little more room to push the sheriff because his irritation with me was like father-daughter as opposed to sheriff-perpetrator. I waited patiently for him to either take my evidence or share what he had. I held out the papers in a my-cards-are-on-the-table sort of way.

He sat forward and leaned his thick forearms on his thighs. His black eye had turned a yellowish-blue color. The man that gave him that had to be drunker than all get-out. Boulder was a large…man. I don't know how else to put it.

"I put up with your little projects and annoyances because of your history. Now, it ain't pity cause you wouldn't want that, and that's not what I give—ever."

He opened his giant hands wide. His palms looked like back catcher's mitts.

"I was close to your mother, as you know, your daddy too in the early days. And of course, who could help but fall in love with the little girl when she arrived?"

I shifted a little uncomfortably in my seat. I cleared my throat even though it didn't need clearing.

"A lot of people talk in this town about those early days. But not me. The past is the past, and I don't like rumors." He exhaled deeply and pushed his large back into the cushion.

"Very few people were there or know the story. All they talk about is your momma's drinking and bar antics. It's a shame."

My throat began to get tight. I didn't want the tears to come. Rage is so much easier than tears.

"So what about the case? The Chrysler 300 and—"

I wiped a tear off my cheek. I wanted to stab myself in the leg for crying in front of the sheriff. His eyebrows went all the way up. When they came back down, his expression changed along with the subject of Momma and my father.

"We don't know if he works for someone or this is the extent of his crew. He—"

And that was it, the sheriff closed up like a clam. He took a long pull on his beer and stared at the can.

"There ain't nothing on that can you haven't read before, Sheriff, drunk or sober. Come on, talk to me," I said.

"A lot happened on freeways when I was Highway patrol, Chloe. A criminal in a vehicle out on the open road gets pulled over. Guess who the lone barrier between him and his freedom is?"

I answered even though the question was rhetorical.

"That's right, us, the CHP. A lot of people in that moment see one bullet to the officer and they're home free. I suspect whoever this asshole is in town right now is tied to my previous days."

"Adds up, seeing as everyone in Bucksville thinks you're the second coming," I said.

"That's a bit of an exaggeration, but—"

"So, do you and your deputies go at him or wait until he makes a move?"

Sheriff Boulder got to his feet. "We do our job. And you, young lady, finish up school and get on with your life."

"Okay, wait, finish school and what was the next part?" I said, pretending to take notes.

He stopped on his way to the kitchen and gave me a sideways look.

"Thanks for stopping by, Chloe. Say hello to Joselyn."

I was up out of my chair. "You can't shut me out, Sheriff. I was verbally assaulted by this Jesse Arlo loser, and I have witnesses. And," I said. "My witness was physically threatened by the guy who verbally harassed me. So, it's not solely police business. It's also my—"

"Did you file a report? Did you come down to the station and file a report?

55

Well, did you?"

"Maybe I'll do that, Jim," I said slowly through clenched teeth. I let myself out.

Chapter Twelve

Most people don't like Mondays. It's back to work, back to the grind with no reprieve until quitting time Friday. I tend to like Mondays. It was usually the day when Momma's 'guest' has to go back to work or grab a Greyhound out of town to *Who-gives-a-shit-ville*, U.S.A.

I made a pot of coffee for Momma for whenever she got up. As I turned from the sink, asshole Brett grabbed me by the shoulders and pinned me against the counter.

"Hey, let go of me, you fuckin—"

"Shh, be nice," he said. He moved his hands to my wrists, squeezed tight, and shoved them against my thighs. His breath was more rank than his B.O.

"Now, listen and listen good cause here's how it's gonna go."

Bam!

I brought my forehead right to the bridge of his nose. I'd never head-butted someone before but I'd seen dozens of videos on it. To my thinking, the main thing was to get my forehead into his nose. If we went forehead to forehead, I'd probably hear ringing bells for weeks. He called me a bitch as he staggered into the fridge. Blood dripped from his cupped hands at the nose. Before he could recover, I had a handful of his greasy hair in my hand and Norma Jean's razor-sharp edge to his throat.

"I won't fucking hesitate," I said. I pushed the blade until more than a trickle of blood ran down his neck. He believed the threat was real.

"Okay, okay," he said.

"What the hell's going on here?" Momma said, making no attempt to close her bathrobe.

"Three guesses, Momma, and you shouldn't need all three."

Momma's eyes turned dark at the corners. "She's my fucking daughter, you asshole."

Momma slapped and punched at him. I tightened the grip on his hair and kept the blade on his throat. Momma kept on smacking and kicking at him as I maneuvered him to the door.

"Open the door, Momma!" I shouted. "Open it!"

She broke from her attack briefly to follow my order, then continued the onslaught, cussing with each blow. Letting the blade off his throat I put my sole to his ass and shove-kicked him hard. He fell down the steps and hit the ground. Momma was like a wolverine after a threat to her cubs but I grabbed her by the waist and yarded her back inside. I slammed the door closed and peered through the blinds while Momma flew into a rage behind me. She slammed every cupboard door and banged every pot within reach.

She was probably angrier at herself for her weakness than actual rage toward the stranger. Good. I wanted her to feel shame. I'd feel sorry for her later but now with adrenaline coursing through my body, I wanted her to feel the guilt of the dammed. I rinsed Norma Jean off in the sink. The Silverado roared to life. He called us stupid bitches and tore off down the drive.

With Norma Jean cleaned and ready for the next episode I checked the time on my phone. I had class in an hour. My hand still shook slightly but I'd be right as rain by the time I put my ass in the seat of A.P. chemistry.

Have I mentioned...fuck my life?

* * *

Hearing the birds' chorus, the beautiful Bucksville day seemed to erase the morning's shit show. The only evidence of loser Brett being on our property was two peel-out tracks made by his truck tires. Oh, and the occasional waft of his B.O. when I walked through the kitchen-living area.

I put my earbuds in and put on Tracy Bonham's first record. Bonham was a big up-and-comer in the '90s, before my time, obviously. She still plays violin, guitar, and sings and is pure badass. Her big hit in the 90s was a song called "Mother Mother," and although was nominated for a Grammy in 1996, she didn't win. Pure bullshit. During the chorus of "Mother Mother" she screams at the top of her lungs, telling her mother 'I'm doing fine.' I find it hilarious and eerily soothing at the same time.

I was about five blocks from school when Kyle fell in beside me.

"Whatcha listening to?"

"Tracy Bonham."

"That's right you gotta thing for her."

"A thing? No, I just like her music," I said.

"Right, you like her shit. That's what I meant." We walked along a bit while Kyle searched for dialog. "Dare I ask how your weekend was?"

I shot him a look.

"That bad, huh? Sorry."

"You don't need to be sorry, it wasn't your fault."

We walked a little further. I was content not to chat at all but the silence was twisting Kyle up in knots.

"What do ya got first? Geography?"

"A.P. chemistry. You?"

"Philosophy."

"Ooh, trees falling in forests with or without sound when a *man* isn't there. So thought provoking," I said.

"Yeah, I guess." He really did have a cute 'aw shucks' smile. Especially since he didn't know it. We came up on the school. A couple of his buddies hollered at him. I'm sure it was important that they have a quick bonding session before hitting class. I think boys need that like us girls need eyeliner and mascara. Who could go longer without, I wonder?

"You better get over there Kyle. They're gonna want to know if you're "hittin' that," I said putting on a deep guy's voice. His laugh was cute too, especially when he feebly tried to deny his buddies were like that. He ran a hand through the thick part of his hair on the top of his head. He had to know it was a sexy move. I bet an ex-girlfriend told him so.

"See you later?" He said.

"It's a small town, so, yeah, chances are, Kyle."

He smiled and jogged over to his tribe. I don't have a tribe. I don't know what they would do or talk about. And I'm sure I'd violate some rule and be ostracized in record time. During my wondrous stay in high school, I've been snickered at, hit on, ignored, invited to join clubs, been considered hot as well as cold, aloof, and bitchy—every scenario on the menu. This tells me nobody knows what the hell they're doing or what's really cool or not. So, I just as well hang out around the perimeter. No lane, just the perimeter.

I pretty much zombie'd my way through the school day. I couldn't shake the morning's incident. This crap was happening far too often. I took the option of taking my last class of the day in the library, where I spent the whole time looking into travel destinations in Europe. Italy and Spain were in a dead heat at the moment. My mind was made up; I'd graduate on a Friday, and I'm gone the following Monday—sooner if Momma's got some new 'friend' over that weekend.

I bolted five minutes before the last bell and headed to Joe's Laundromat. Joe's is my part-time gig. The gig itself is easy and doesn't pay great. However, I convinced Joe English, the boss, into taking in people's laundry and cleaning it for them for extra cash. Joe balked at first but he let me run with it and it turned a tidy—pun intended—little profit. Seeing as Momma didn't raise no fool, I arranged a fifty percent cut for me out of the deal. But the real cash is in the tips I make. Most of the business comes from the construction workers. By week's end, their gear is filthy. Do you think they want to spend minute-one doing laundry when there are perfectly good bars open? Hell to the no. They drop the laundry, go get their buzz on, come back and tip the light-skinned brown girl like she was a dancer in a gentlemen's club. The locals are also good tippers—another perk of small-town generosity.

Skinny Dave, or Skinny as everyone calls him split the second I showed up to relieve him of his shift. This was pretty much on the regular. Skinny plays some sort of online video game with like-minded losers. So when I show up at 3:45-ish he's got one leg on his mountain bike pedal when I walk through the door.

The first thing I do after quick greetings to customers doing their own laundry is change the music from Skinny's to mine. People tend to appreciate it. Skater-punk isn't for everybody. I then check the drop-off laundry. After going through the list of desired temperatures, detergents, and fabric softeners I get the machines rumbling. With hands gloved up to my biceps like a hazmat worker, I sort faster than a Vegas blackjack dealer shuffles cards. No need to smell or examine what people need cleaned. Get it in the washer, slam the door home, and hit go!

With that done, I'll clean and tidy a bit, empty lint trays, sweep the floor—the stuff a monkey could do. Then the earbuds go in, and a book comes out. I usually go with whatever the current recommendation is from actress Reese Witherspoon's book club list. Today would be different. I wanted to dig deeper into Jesse Arlo. I barely had the search engine open when one of his crew members walked in. It was the one who never said a word when they braced sheriff Boulder. If ever cornered in a back alley, he'd be the one that would give me the most concern. Even with Norma Jean and a good night's sleep prior, I wouldn't see myself walking out of that alley alive. I also have no doubt that if Sheriff Boulder was forced to draw on those guys, the 'quiet one' would be target one.

He wore what some call a denim tuxedo: faded blue jeans and a jean jacket to match. Well defined muscles rippled and rolled in a tight black t-shirt beneath the jacket. He was scarier with his sunglasses off than on. It wasn't the orangey eye color, but it was the way they were almost all-knowing. Like a demon in a horror movie that knows your thoughts; even the ones you haven't had yet. Half of his lip curled up when our eyes met. He moved to the nearest washing machine and stared at the controls.

"Can I help you, sir?" My voice was croaky, but he didn't know me so hopefully, he couldn't detect how freaked out I was.

He turned to me and gave me a quick shake 'no' of the head. His eyes moved back to the machine. In an extremely quick move, he tore off his jean jacket. I think I flinched. The jacket went into the washer. The door slammed behind it. He walked toward me and stopped five feet from where I stood.

"Detergent," he said. It sounded part question, part command.

"End of this row. Dollar-seventy-five a pack. A quarter pack will do your—"

He stalked past, not needing the detergent-to-load ratio. I spied his sinewy back as he walked by. His body seemed built for violence, inflicting pain. I felt my cheeks and scalp heat up. He was in town for Sheriff Boulder, and clearly, he was the enforcer of the group. It didn't take much to imagine he was in charge of torture if his boss needed it done. And here he was in my place of business…in my town. So what if I can't wait to bail on this town and never look back. I'm here now—with Norma Jean.

When he walked back I got a whiff of his cologne. It was clean like soap, not fruity or spicy. He added detergent, quarters then leaned against the machine with his back to it. Vascular forearms folded across his chest. He stared straight ahead. Who knew what his thoughts were? For the first time, I realized the other patrons had left. There was just me and the guy I decided to call the Quiet One. It was like being in a room with a poisonous snake. Just because you knew where the snake was didn't make it any more comfortable.

If he put the wash on the short cycle he'd be there twenty-eight minutes. And if he used one of the higher-end dryers, he'd be out fifteen minutes after that. I checked the time on my phone. I tried to get back to my search of his greasy boss, but I couldn't relax. I felt like he'd know what I was searching for—freaking demon. The wash reached the spin cycle when he came down the row and leaned against the counter opposite me.

At this distance, I pinpointed another feature that made my skin slither: his haircut. His bangs were short-longish, but he had a stupid part that pulled a portion of his bangs to the side like—

My god, he looks like the bad guy in No Country For Old Men. *What was his—ah, Javier Bardem.*

All of a sudden, I felt like I slipped into an ice bath and the water level was about to cover my head.

"I don't want to freak you out. Never want to freak any woman out, but yer Chloe Savannah, ain't you?"

"You think opening with a sentence like that will put a girl at ease?"

His lip curled up, then right back down. "Fair point."

I didn't push the conversation. Anything I said would be more info for him. I'm fine and dandy with uncomfortable silences. Deputy Tawanna once said, 'white men talk a lot because they fear the silence, and as a result they only hear themselves.' He lowered his eyes to Norma at my hip.

"Colombia River knife, five and a half-inch blade. Partially serrated edge."

The Quiet One was right on the money. And he read all that just from Norma's hilt. Still, it didn't mean I had words for him. He didn't seem to need them.

"I know how it must look. City guys in a muscle car. Clearly, we ain't tourists."

I decided to talk in case I was holding my breath. "Your jacket will be done in five minutes, give or take. The Kenmores are our fastest dryers. F.Y.I."

He nodded.

"The sheriff seems like a decent man. D'ya like him?"

"I like just about everyone who lives in this town. Tourists I can do without. Not to mention drifters and passers-through," I said. "I've got no time for them. I gotta get back to work."

I had to walk past him to get to my client's clothes. I held my breath and pulled my shoulders back. I walked tall with every muscle coiled at the ready. He gave a 'huh' sound as I passed.

"You know Jim Boulder used to be a chippy, a C.H.P. officer," he said.

I pulled a load from the washer, and as I jammed it into the dryer, I envisioned stuffing his body into a trunk or that very dryer, maybe. I slammed the door shut, set the timer, and started it up. The only thing that makes me uncomfortable in this shit world is men. And here was another one putting the fear into me. I took a deep breath and let it out slowly. I walked toward him with no real plan except to let him know that even though he made me want to cry out for help, I'd face him woman to man. If his plan was to hurt me, he'd better get on with it. And if I couldn't get Norma to him, I'd scratch at least one of his orange tabby eyes out.

I picked up the cologne scent again. He was short for a man but still had two inches on me.

"Listen, bud, if you tangle with Boulder, it ends with you catching a bullet.

If you fuck with me, you also get a bullet, even if you kill me here and now."

He tilted his head to the side as if studying an unknown species. He pushed off the counter. He was behind me before I knew where he was. I stayed sculpture still. He slow- walked around me as if I were a car in a showroom. Once his three-sixty-degree lap was done, he leaned close.

"You're high-strung, Chloe. Maybe you oughta put some smooth jazz in them ear buds."

I didn't chance moving for Norma, he was too quick. Besides, I'd been around enough of Momma's losers to know that this was the cat toying with the mouse part. He wasn't going to do anything here. Still, I almost thought I might pee my pants. I did another slow in and out of oxygen, then spoke.

"When your jacket's done, I think you should leave," I said. "Just...fucking... leave." My sculpture-still body began to tremble slightly.

"Whoa, where's that small-town hospitality I've heard so much—"

"Is there a problem here?" I hadn't heard Kyle walk in.

"Whoa, easy, Kyle," the Quiet One said.

"Who the fuck are you? And what are you doing to my girl? She's obviously upset." Kyle got between me and the Quiet One. I didn't want that—sort of didn't.

"Your girl?" the Quiet One said. Hearing Kyle's declaration, my eyebrows threatened to rise, but I held my impassive yet shaky expression.

"I heard what she said. When your shit is done, do yourself a favor and beat it," Kyle ordered.

The Quiet One was in front of Kyle in two strides so quick he appeared to float as if on a segue. Kyle held his ground, but I wouldn't say on steady legs. A piece of paper would barely have fit between their faces. My thumb went to Norma Jean.

"Do you hear that, asshole?" the Quiet One said, holding up an index finger.

"Yeah, what's that?" Kyle asked.

"My wash is done."

Kyle seemed as surprised as I was by the beeping washer. I hadn't heard it go off. He stepped around Kyle and hauled his jacket out of the wash, and fired up a Kenmore.

"I'll come back when it's dry. Give Kyle and his gal a chance to talk about proms and hayrides, or whatever boring shit y'all do out here."

"Yeah, bite me, dude," Kyle said. I'd never let on, but I noticed a slight sheen of sweat on Kyle's forehead…and our A.C. was on full blast.

It took us about fifteen minutes to thaw out from the Quiet One's movie. We settled into our easiest dialog to date. Kyle helped me fold clothes, or rather, I taught him how to do it. We gossiped a little, he brought me up to speed on what and who I should follow on Instagram. He even tried to talk me into joining TikTok.

"Not in a million years, Kyle. I can barely stomach the gram."

"I'll help you. Give me a day, and I'll have you laughing at funny shit and crying over puppy videos."

I stopped folding a pair of kakis. "Who in the hell wants to cry at puppies? You're so extra."

"I meant cry laughing, they're so cute."

Time seemed to speed up around Kyle. It seemed so normal, which with Momma's leches and the psycho Quiet One was a welcome dalliance—depending on where it went, of course. Social media talk led to mild flirtation. Kyle seemed to be in his stride, like he'd slid on a new pair of shoes that fit to a T. All awkwardness gone. Before I knew it, we were leaning in for our first kiss—in a laundromat, no less!

"Aw, that's so sweet," the Quiet One said on his return.

I went from turned-on to freezing cold in the ice bath again in seconds. Kyle and I jumped apart, startled. Kyle made a move toward the intruder, but I grabbed him by his biceps.

"Don't," I said.

The demon eased into his jean jacket. "Ooh, nice and toasty."

"Move on, asshole," Kyle said.

"I'm movin', tough guy. Chloe, please say hi to yer Jim Boulder there."

This time Kyle held me back. "You better not fuck with my sheriff!"

"Ya hear that, Kyle? Boulder is *her* sheriff. Geez, I wonder if the big sheriff was on her mind when she was about to lip lock with ya?"

The denim tuxedo and its crooked smiling passenger eased out the door.

The mood was done for both Kyle and me.

"Who is that asshole, and how does he know our names?"

"Easy enough to ask people in a town like this. He doesn't know us. He's just fucking with us. There's a difference," I said. "He and his toy posse are here for the sheriff for some reason."

"Well, I hope you stay out of it, Chloe. I know how you can be. Please let the police handle it."

I went back to bagging up a load of folded clothes.

"What is it with you and everybody? When a man interferes or steps into the shit, no one warns him away. It's just accepted that a man's gotta do what a man's gotta do, bullshit. But when a woman brings something to the table or has an idea or wants to help out the sheriff of her town, it's 'stand down, Chloe, stand aside and let the big boys take over.' Screw that." I said. "And people wonder why I want to leave this fuck hole."

"We just don't want to see you get hurt."

I flashed him a look that would drop a heavyweight boxer. He raised his hands up in surrender.

"I know that sounds cliche and lame, but if these guys are after Boulder, I'm sure he knows about it, and he's got deputies. If it's bigger than that, he can call in the Feds. His gang is bigger than four guys rolling around in a 300," he said.

I pulled the drawstring tight on the laundry bag and stored it with the others.

"I get it, but it's still a double standard."

Kyle moved close and took my face in his hands. He kissed me lightly on the forehead. "So, will you stay out of it? For me?"

I pulled away. His question, not to mention the timing, pissed me off. "I'll do whatever it is I decide to do. Just like a man doin' what he's got to do."

I walked to the back office as if I had something to take care of. "Thanks for your help with that guy. Maybe I'll see you tomorrow at school." When I emerged five minutes later, Kyle was gone. At least he could take a hint.

* * *

I get the phrase 'shit rolls downhill,' but I think it needs to be amended because to me, shit is everywhere. And my life is smack-dab in the middle of it. I didn't have it in me to deal with Momma's crap when I got home, but sure enough…

"Momma, wake up. Wake up," I said. The third slap pulled her from the depths.

"Huh? What? Why you hittin' me?" Her eyes stayed shut as she asked.

"Because you puked on your bathrobe, again. And I'm not cleaning you up. Too fucking tired."

"I used to change your diapers, girl!" She was up out of her chair so fast you might have thought she'd been fake sleeping.

"Did I forget to say thank you? Thank you for being a mother seventeen years ago. Please clean yourself up. You stink," I said.

"Your attitude stinks. How you tre—treat me stinks, Chl—Chloe. I'm your mother."

"I've had it, Joselyn! I'm your daughter, but I'm the one looking after you. And you wanna talk treatment? Your asshole drunk whatever they ares would like to treat me like a two-dollar whore. So don't come at me with your drunken busted violin of bullshit."

She came at me fast with her hand raised. I caught her hand easily long before the slap connected.

"Is that it? You gonna slap me into loving you? What's up with you?" I said, tossing her hand aside and moving to the couch.

"He didn't call," she said. She plopped down on the lounger and put her face in her hands. "He said he'd call. May—maybe get off work early and come by, but he's just like the rest, goddamit. Why?" She screamed the last word.

I kept my voice barely above a whisper. "*That's* what's set you off? That loser who's been up in you and wanted your daughter next—he—that's what's got you all drunk and stupid up in here? Because he didn't call?"

"I'm all alone!" she screamed. "You don't get it. I'm all alone! Your father's gone, I have no friends—hell, you might as well be gone the way you look at me. If looks could kill, Chloe, I'd be in pine box…unless you just buried me in the ya—yard in this fucking pukey robe!" She broke down and sobbed. I gave her a full minute before getting up from the couch. I walked to her and put a gentle hand on her back.

"You're not entirely alone, Joselyn," I said. "But come June 17th, you will be. I'm going to Europe, and you, well, you can do whatever your little dead heart desires."

She sobbed harder as I walked back to my room. I didn't even feel sad for Momma. In fact, I felt like a freshly minted billionaire because I'd finally made a choice. No more sitting on the fence of should I stay or go. I was liberated. Isn't that what the self help books would call it?

Chapter Thirteen

Momma drank and pouted in her room for the rest of the night. After my knife throws and a little carving, I tip-toed through TikTok. After two dance videos, a strange-looking emu animal thing, and watching an epic fail of some goof on a skateboard I was done. I sacked out.

Nope, still not joining that shit.

Momma was up before me the next day. Coffee was on, breakfast of hash browns and fried eggs sizzled in the pan, and the place was damn near spotless. Sunlight streaked through the shutters. If it started and ended there, this might have been the opening to a cute little movie. Momma's face had some color to it, and the way the sun streamed in the kitchen window and kissed her cheek made her look a decade younger.

"Morning, sweetheart. Hungry?"

She was already plating before I could answer. I sat. I indulged. I played the good daughter, but I was warier than an aging dog at a kill shelter. Momma did this on occasion. She'd dust herself off, shower, splash on a bit of face paint, and clean house. Next would come the promise of going cold turkey. This would be followed by two or three days of good behavior before the bottle would call her back home.

"Smells good, Momma," *said the good daughter.*

After pleasant small talk to nowhere, Momma cleared her throat in preparation for a speech. The speech. It was like countless dozens before it, so I'll spare you the long version. Short version is: I love you, I'm sorry, I'm trying, one day at a time...yada yada blah blah bullshit. I finished up and thanked Momma for a wonderful meal. Before I got out of my seat, she was up.

"Oh, let me," she said. She grabbed my plate and rinsed it in the sink. When I was young, the dry-out spells filled me with hope like an endless pitcher of sweet tea spilling down my gullet. Problem was when drunk Joselyn returned, the pitcher would crash to the floor and break into a million pieces leaving me to clean up the sticky mess. Unless I wanted an army of ants for roommates. Nowadays, I remain pleasant and wait for the other bottle to drop. Being that it was Tuesday I figured I'd have peace and cleanliness until, oh, Friday morning, Friday night maybe.

Ah, the tranquility before the tempest.

* * *

I walked my usual route home from school and was about to enter Saul's Bakery when Deputy Raven Tawanna pulled up beside me in the sheriff's S.U.V. She rolled the window down.

"Hey, Chloe."

"Officer Bad Ass, how are you?"

"Stop that crap. Get in."

We drove a half block until Raven pulled into a parking spot between an Audi A7 and a blue and white '90s Chevy pickup truck. She put the Ford in park and turned her body at an angle to face me. Her thick black braid rested over her shoulder and ran down to her biceps.

"You meddle," she said. "And I don't have the energy to shove you off."

I took a page from her book and waited for my time to speak. Her eyes moved to Norma Jean on my hip then back to lock with mine.

"Sheriff Boulder told me of your interest in our visitors."

I nodded but held my silence.

"You're a nosy little—so...what have you got?"

"I tip-toed around the web and found the 300 belongs to the one that acts like the boss." I kept going and fed her what I was going to feed Boulder.

"That's about what I got on the guy. They're staying at The Rueben Motel off the 17 Freeway. I've been sitting on them when my time allows it," the deputy said. That put them in the neighboring town of Moreford.

"And you want me to watch them when you can't," I said. I could have kicked myself for blurting like a pre-teen.

"Shit, no, Chloe, you're not a cop, and these guys are bad news. I can feel it."

"So, what have you seen?"

"Each has his own room. They pretty much lay low at night, although the boss picked up a chick I didn't recognize. She was probably from Moreford county. Anyway, she stayed the night."

I told her about my interaction with the Quiet One at the laundromat. She liked the name I gave him and agreed he's probably the most dangerous one. She was basing this on what I gave her as well as what Boulder had told her.

"What do you think they want with Boulder?" I asked.

"They may not necessarily want anything with him specifically."

"It looked that way to me at the creek, not to mention the Quiet One asked me about the sheriff as well."

"I think they're here for a job. Maybe a bank, home invasion, armored car, something like that. They've got the look."

"Then how do you explain the Boulder angle?" I asked.

She didn't answer right away. Just stared out the truck window.

Finally, "Oftentimes when guys would pull bank jobs they'd not only case the place but specifically the armed guard or guards. Were they left handed or right? Did they look brave or the type to freeze when things got hot? What were their reflexes like? Stuff like that."

She clammed up again so I jumped in. "So they could be testing the sheriff's mettle and see if he'll be a problem when they pull the job. Hmm."

She still hadn't spoken, so I kept going.

"Maybe, but I don't know, Raven. It seemed kinda personal to me."

"Yeah, the sheriff elaborated on your little hide and seek game at the creek."

I felt like an older sister was scolding me. It didn't bring me down in any way. I've got nothing but the utmost respect for Raven Tawanna—officer Bad Ass.

"Right place at the right time was all. Look, I think they're here for the sheriff and I think it's from his past. Maybe his C.H.I.P. days."

"Anything's possible, and we're in the early stages here."

"*We're* in the early stages?" I smiled. "You said we're…just sayin'."

She shot me a cool sideways look. "I don't like you being in this at all, and Boulder would have my hide if he knew I was talking to you."

"But you like me," I said.

"Grow up. You're stubborn. I know there's no backing you off, like I said."

She fired up the engine, which I took as my cue the meeting was over. I opened the door and put one foot on the running board.

"You know who else is stubborn, Officer Bad Ass?" I pointed my index finger at her.

"That's right. And it's why I like you," she said. "Keep Norma sharp and get the fuck out of my truck before I arrest you for being annoying."

I stepped out and closed the door.

"Be safe cause if you get hurt, Boulder will kill me, then I'll have to kill you."

"That doesn't really make sense, Officer Bad A—"

Her tires squealed as she pulled back away from the curb.

Chapter Fourteen

I had my hand on the door handle to the bakery and was about to enter when I heard the rumble of a muscle car. It was no big reach to guess who was nosing its way down the block. I looked over my shoulder. Henchman number two from the day before who'd catcalled me and harassed me the day before made his hand into a pistol and fired a shot at me. Dick. I gave him my middle finger. Then had an idea.

Ten minutes later I was home and out of breath. I didn't bother checking on Momma. She was either still on the wagon or not. She could wait. I hopped in my truck and turned her over. Deputy Tawanna mentioned the motel the little gang was staying at. I thought, why not do a little surveillance of my own? Why mention it if she didn't want me to take a peek at the interlopers? She'd said she had limited time for surveillance after all. She was baiting me like a fly fisherman with a nymph fishing lure. Although the fish gets a hook in the mouth so I'd need to be super careful.

I was fairly certain the losers would still be rolling around town doing whatever it is they do, so why not check the lay of the land? The drive out to the Rueben Motel was picturesque. The part dirt, part blacktop was windy and framed by what I call mini sequoias. I sometimes drove this road just to air out thoughts or take a break from Momma. The town of Moreford was only a fifteen-minute trip from Bucksville. My tank was at three-quarters so I bypassed the tiny three-pump gas station on the way in. Jed, the station owner's fourteen-year-old son stopped pushing a broom and gave me a quick wave as I went by. I waved and gave him a double-tap of the horn. It's rude not to honk at people you know in these parts.

The Reuben Motel was built to look like a giant barn, with red cedar siding and large barn-style entry doors. It must have been someone's idea of a country welcome. I drove past and took a side road, made a left, and came around from behind the building. The Chrysler 300 was nowhere in sight. In fact, occupancy looked darn near empty. That could mean guests were out for the day hiking, shopping or wine tasting. I pulled into a spot at the back of the motel directly beside the side road for a quick exit.

I wore a pair of my mid-rise boot-cut jeans. I strapped Norma Jean to my dark leather belt and slid my smaller Bowie, The Girl, into my front pocket. More on her later. The metal handle clipped to the pocket lip. I wore my dark tan suede cowboy boots, which may not have been best for a quick getaway but they were golden for kicking men in the nuts, not to mention stomping…should it come to that. I had on a navy blue cap sleeve, tissue-thin t-shirt and over that my brown suede three-quarter length blazer. I wore it unbuttoned for ease of movement.

The entrance door squeaked on its hinges as I walked in. WD-40 would fix the problem in a pinch but they probably left it as-is to alert the clerk to arriving guests. The woman behind the counter was mid-sixties and wore an oven-warm customer service smile.

"Welcome to the Rueben. How can I help you, young lady?"

I decided to go direct. "I wonder if you could tell me about a few of your guests. They drive a black Chrysler 300."

Her smile slipped into a frown. "Oh, sugar, I can't give out information about our guests, it would be against policy."

"I understand. I really don't know how to go about this stuff because I'm just—well anyway. Here," I said. I pulled a folded twenty out of my back pocket. I had it all planned out on the way over.

She took the twenty faster than a frog's tongue nabs a fly. The 'country welcome' demeanor dropped from her face and body language.

"How can I help?" she said.

"I think they're trouble. I live just over in Bucksville and we've always been friendly neighbors, us and Moreford." She nodded in agreement. This was good.

"I believe they might be up to something neither one of our little towns would approve of. Have you seen anything suspicious or—?"

"Well, I don't know. What do you mean by suspicious?"

I realized I didn't really know myself. "How 'bout you tell me about their habits I guess." I forced a giggle to imply the 'innocent kid trying to do right' schtick. I hoped she'd see the two of us as a couple of small-town ladies trying to protect our homes and loved ones.

"I don't like them, I can tell you that. Word is they spend most nights at the Horse and Buggy Bar. They've had a few close calls stirring up trouble but nothing major. No big brawls or anything."

"Have they said how long they're staying?" I asked.

"Nope. They paid for three days up front. Each of them has his own room. Then just this morning they paid for another three days."

Oh great.

I couldn't think of any more questions, this not really being my thing and all. I hauled out my phone.

"Do you have a cell phone? I'd like to text you my number, you know, in case you think of anything else or hear something."

She scrunched her eyebrows. "Wouldn't it be quicker to write it down? Here," she said and handed me a yellow post-it paper and pen. I hesitated and she picked up on it.

"You're worried they might see your name on the post-it if I lose it. Let's give you a code name then. How 'bout Colombia River, the brand of that blade on your hip under that lovely blazer of yours."

"I knew I liked you, uh, I'm so sorry I forgot to get your name. I'm Chloe."

"Emmylou. And I knew I liked you when I saw the cutlery you carry." She touched her own jeans pocket indicating The Girl, my folding pocket knife. The tried and true Bowie knife.

"I've got something for you." She reached under the counter and laid a leather-handled Buck knife with a seven-inch blade on the counter.

"Dang sakes, Emmylou, that thing is bigger than you are."

She smiled proudly as if introducing her newborn child. She didn't say anything. Her newborn needed no words.

"Honestly, I don't know how you wield that thing, but…may I?"

"By all means, sugar."

I picked up the knife and checked its weight. I closed one eye and looked down the blade. I did a few slow forehand and backhand slashes, then I laid it flat on my palm.

"Balanced like a prize fighter's diet," I said. "I couldn't toss this sword five feet, but—"

"But with a two-handed plunge, you'll get through ribs, cartilage, and the flesh of a three hundred pound man," she grinned. "It's got what I like to call stopping power, Chloe."

"You're one dark horse of a bitch, Emmylou."

"Ha! I am at that," she said. She took the knife back and returned it to its home.

"Thank you for your time Emmylou, this has been fun in a way."

She pulled the twenty I gave her from her bra strap and placed it on the counter.

"Keep it," she said. "You'll need it to buy a drink if you plan on blending in over at the Horse and Buggy. I'm assuming that's now a destination of yours?"

"Uh, yeah, I guess, but you keep the twenty. I like your style."

"And I yours. Not taking your money, honey," she said. I could see there was no persuading her.

"Chloe, you need to be twenty-one to get into the joint but you're cuter than a kitten's whiskers so I don't think you'll have a problem."

"Thanks, Emmylou."

"Nothing of it. Keep your blades sharp and keep 'em close."

* * *

The Horse and Buggy had an old wooden buggy and horse sculpture in the parking lot. Ooh aah, the level of creativity was staggering. The parking lot was heavily populated with trucks, which would be mostly locals. In addition, there were foreign S.U.V.s, a few motorcycles, and the occasional

Japanese sedan.

With each step closer to the bar my heart seemed to want to bust out of my rib cage. I didn't care if I got I.D.'d, it was that annoying voice of doubt in my head screaming, 'what do you think you're doing Chloe? These guys are dangerous men.' Still, my boots scuffed their way toward the H and B bar. Heel, toe, heel toe.

"Can I help you, sweetheart?" The bouncer was bigger than Sheriff Boulder and twenty years younger. His muscles bulged all over his torso, fighting to get out of his tight black Nike fitness shirt. I wondered if his day job was weight lifting—just straight-up lifting.

"Just meeting a girlfriend for a drink," I smiled. I almost said it as a question—such a dork.

"You twenty-one?"

"Twenty-two, actually."

His grin let us both know he knew I was bullshitting. But judging how long he took in the view of my chest I knew I was golden, so long as he didn't expect anything.

"If the law shows up, I'll tell them you showed me I.D. If your real I.D. says you're under age, I'll tell them you must have shown me a fake one and tossed it."

"Thanks, Tyler," I said, looking at the name tag on his shirt. However, I only glanced at his chest. He stood aside so I could enter. He spoke to my back.

"You're young and hot. Don't get in over your head."

A compliment with a touch of the paternal—interesting. I turned and gave him a salute and a smile.

"By the way, I'd normally take that off you but seeing as…"

His eyes went to Norma Jean on my hip. I'd forgotten all about her.

"Thanks, Tyler, you're a good dude." I figured that's what he and his buddies call each other at the bench press.

Heads turned when I walked in, but I know that's what happens at bars. Especially with blue-collar workers. They wonder if the new thing walking in is hot, and if so will she be their plaything. I weaved through the tables and high tops and headed straight for the bar. I'm not a big drinker for obvious reasons. But working men's eyes lingered on my ass a little too long for comfort, so some sort of wine cooler was definitely going to happen.

The bartender was a tatted-up dusty blond with fake thirty-eight D's. I never care either way if girls get fake boobs, but I must say, although large, they worked for this bartender. Her sunshiny smile and bounce in her step read comfortable-confidence. And her numerous tip jars spilling over, mostly with twenties, said this chick had these dudes' numbers.

Go 'head, girl.

"Well, hello, pretty thing. What'll ya have?"

Her jasmine perfume was applied a little too heavily. But I'm sure it was a necessity if she wanted it to cut through testosterone, dirt, and grease in the place. Her tattoos were mostly the sunflower and Buddha-type gentle tats. Peaceful tats, hostile environment. Grace under pressure. I liked her immediately.

"What's en vogue as far as wine coolers these days?" I asked.

"Truly's number one. White Claw's a close second. And we got 'em both."

"Let's go with number one."

"Goin' with a winner, nice," she winked. "Comin' right up, beautiful."

As Lucy, according to her tag, moved her shapely hips down the bar, more than half the guys leaned in for the show. I took a moment to scan the place and couldn't believe my eyes or luck. And I mean dumb luck.

"This is what ya call fate, little girl," said the mixed-raced henchman from the Chrysler 300. I'm an expert on the smell of booze, thanks to Momma. I had to lean way back because this guy'd been drinking since dawn or whenever his kind rose from sleep.

"Fate, how?" I was stalling for time. I needed my heartbeat to slow down. His eyes danced between focused and unfocused as he tried to get a bead on me.

"Look," he said. "I wanna 'pologize for the other...for...with the car. It was rude." He smiled, but his gaze was a hair to my left.

"Apology accepted." I was coming around now.

"Good. That's good. Cause I'm really not...not a bad guy."

78

I felt like digging. Maybe I'd get something for the sheriff. Momma can never keep a secret when she's loaded, so—

"So, what brings you guys to these parts?" I smiled as best I could while practically doing a gymnastic move to keep away from his stench.

"Oh, just a little va–vacay."

I tilted my head to the side like a primary school teacher that's just heard a lie.

"Come on, level with me. I promise I won't tell," I said. "Let's start with your name."

"Carter. I'm Carter."

I waited for him to continue.

"The boss is Jesse, and he's awesome, by the way, and our big dummy is Blocker, like…like in football."

"Nice. Anyone else?" I asked. I wanted the Quiet One's name.

"Nope," he said and blinked. "Wait, one more, but he's weird. I don't wanna talk about him."

I'd come back to him.

"Do you have business with Sheriff Boulder?" I asked.

He frowned at me. Maybe I went too fast. He swayed forward and back before being forced to re-focus on me. A creepy smile spread on his face.

"Boulder and business. Business…business and Boulder. I guess you could call it that. Ya see, he's been a bad boy. Was, was a bad…is a bad—"

He slumped forward and hit his head on the bar but bounced up like nothing happened. His eyes searched for me, but it was moot. Tyler, the bouncer, moved in and hefted him off the barstool like he was moving a five-ounce bag of potato chips.

"That's it, bud. Let's call it."

"Hey, hey, I'm talking to the hot little…hot little thing there."

He didn't put up a struggle. I checked the bar and didn't see his crew anywhere, so I turned back to my drink. I'm not sure how he did it, but by the time I set the drink back on the bar, the Jesse Arlo eased onto the barstool beside me. His blazer was either at his table or in the 300, or maybe the motel. Regardless he now just wore a black button-up collared shirt that had a slight, almost satiny sheen to it. Up close, he freaked me out because was an absolute hottie. I did my best not to show it.

"Hello, you," he said. His teeth were bleached by lasers and sat in Hollywood-level perfect rows. His natural skin tone was dark, maybe Latino or indigenous, but it had also been kissed by the sun. I had every reason to hate the man, but my body was betraying me. My heart fluttered, my pits sweated, and my face flushed. All the things that happen when I'm horny. W.T.F.? I had movie flashes of us doing it. Those thick hands exploring my body, and my body tingling with each touch.

God knows what I would have suggested right then and there if his smile hadn't given it all away. It was the type of smile that had not only been practiced, it would be the same smile he'd wear during foreplay as he would kicking a puppy in the ribs. I could just tell. There was just the slightest hint of sadism behind soft brown eyes, which were effing gorgeous, by the way. The cruelty that danced behind the mysterious curtain and the fact he was in town to mess with Boulder was enough for me to break the spell...thank god!

"Ah, your friend just got tossed, aren't you gonna—"

He waved his hand and briefly looked over his shoulder. "Ah, he's inebriated, and those are the consequences." He slid his stool close to mine. My body threatened to betray me again. Lucky for me, Lucy came to the rescue.

"What can I get ya?" she asked. The ring leader didn't get the friendly Lucy that I got.

"Bourbon, your good stuff. Double please and another Truly for the young lady."

Lucy looked at me.

"No, I'm good, thank you."

"Nah, I insist," he said. "Look, my loser buddy obviously did or said something stupid, and I want to make it up to you. Please."

His smile was melting away my force field.

"No, really, it's—"

"My mother always said a man should be allowed to apologize. If for no

80

other reason, another man might hear it and pick up on the practice."

"Your mother said all that?" I asked.

"Mm-hmm."

"The lady said she was fine," Lucy interrupted. "Are you always this good a listener?"

"Okay. Okay, I won't persist, as I come in peace. Just the bourbon then."

"No," I blurted. "I mean, no it's okay. I'll take another Truly, Lucy. Thank you."

Lucy held a moment, then moved down the bar with a walk full of pissed-off reluctance. I hope I hadn't lost my ally. I shocked myself by ordering a second drink but felt I needed to keep the asshole…gorgeous asshole talking.

The top two buttons of his shirt were undone, and a pair of sunglasses sat at the upper chest. The sleeves were rolled up, revealing forearms of veins and sinew. I already covered the hands part. His dress pants were probably four times the price of Dockers and fit as if tailored. He took both strong hands and ran them through his thick dark locks. He had done the move at the creek when he met the sheriff. It was obviously a move to bring attention to his thick hair. But I must say, seeing it up close—it worked.

I told myself I wasn't staring but rather paying close attention to detail. His grin told me another thing: he knew I liked what I saw.

Dang it!

Lucy put our drinks down and looked him dead in the eye. His charms didn't gain an inch of purchase. Lucy no doubt had seen it a thousand times working in a place like the Horse and Buggy. I wanted a bit of her in me when I grew up. She didn't alter her expression one iota when she told him what he owed. He pulled a money clip from his front pocket and counted off bills without moving his eyes from hers. Once the money added up, he tossed an extra twenty onto the pile as a tip. Lucy's thank you was the back corner of a deep freeze—cold.

"The other day, my associate howled at you like a college kid on spring break. I want to apologize for that too. Good help is a killer…to find."

He raised his glass and held it halfway between us. I slowly raised mine and clinked his glass. I was ten different forms of uncomfortable. I get angry when that happens, so I got right to it.

"Why are you here in town? What do you want with the sheriff?"

"Whoa, slow down darlin'. We're just having a drink, you and me."

The smile was permanent.

"So that's it? Ya lock up until I tell you my business, is that it?" He asked.

I nodded. He took a sip of his bourbon and let out an exaggerated 'ah' sound. I knew what this was. He was trying to take the dominant position in the conversation. Long pause, drink, hot smile. Fuck him. I studied this in my psych course. Dude was an amateur. This was good. His ego was large, and so, his overconfidence was something I could use.

I took a sip of my drink and faked a cough as if it went down the wrong side. He came close and asked if I was all right. Now he got to play the concerned hero. He reached over the bar, grabbed a clean glass, and poured me some water from the water gun. Lucy frowned from the far end of the bar.

"Thank you," I said, accepting the glass. I was now the weak damsel, and he saved me.

"So, tell me why you're here again?" I said once I recovered.

He sat back and ran his hands through his hair again. Why not tell the hot young chick your plans? She's obviously harmless. She can't possibly be a threat of any kind.

Keep telling yourself that, asshole.

Jesse Arlo turned sideways on his stool and rest his loafer on the foot rail. He looked at me as if studying, but I could tell this was a move he used with women. Put them slightly off kilter with a gaze of interest while holding back dialog just prior to the point of the uncomfortable. It was meant to show the woman he was attracted to them and that they had his undivided attention.

I channeled my inner Deputy Tawanna, the proud Chickasaw, and settled in for a staring contest as long as it would take. I could do this all day.

"You showed me something on the street that day. You've got grit. You don't take any shit," he said. "A strong woman is an attractive woman, Chloe. Although not all men are up for the task, so screw 'em."

He took a measured sip of his drink. When he placed the drink back on the bar, he leaned closer.

"Everybody has a past, Chloe. Mine is a little longer than yours and the sheriff's longer than mine. Some of us have checkered pasts. Unsightly. Ugly. Even sinful. For that, there must be an accounting. The universe keeps score, isn't that what the yogis say?"

"The universe keeps score, or man keeps score?" I said.

He allowed a brief smile before pressing on.

"You live with your mother. Just the two of you."

Now you've stepped up to the line.

"I'm sure you love your mother," he said. A shadow passed over his eyes as he spotted my discomfort. "The girl who wouldn't take shit from the hollerin' asshole in my 300 would probably do anything for her mother."

And then he put on a charming smile that said he understood me, and in fact, we were kindred on this point. It was criminal the good looks bestowed upon this man.

"Family. We do what needs to be done for family. Especially our mothers." He raised his glass in a toast. He didn't wait for me to cheer, knowing I had no intention of doing so. He took a tiny sip of his drink and set the tumbler on the bar.

"You know your illustrious Sheriff Boulder might not be as saintly as the good people of Bucksville think."

"Really?" I said, adding a fake half-cough.

"He's got a past, sweetheart, like we all do." He took another sip but didn't keep up with the dialog. Time to prompt.

"So we all have a past. What's the big deal, then?"

He shifted another quarter turn on his stool, and quickly inched toward me.

"Because the lawman has crossed the line. He thought himself above the law," he said. "At least one time that I know of."

I sat back and folded my arms. All of the sex appeal he'd mustered earlier had drifted with the passing clouds. He was a bully, and like any typical bully, all you need to do is find that nerve ending and put your boot heel to it. Handsome, sexy Josh Brolin look-a-like is history.

"Wow, this kinda sounds like a western movie. Band of ruffians rides into town in hemi-loaded Chrysler to even the score with the town sheriff."

He screwed up his face as if wondering where the helpless coughing girl disappeared to? He studied me. I didn't need my psych course to study him. I'd already written the exam and gotten an A. This guy was a B-movie loser.

"What's your game, sweetheart?"

It was my turn to lean in. When I did, I noticed Lucy ease in our direction—same as Tyler, the bouncer.

"This ain't no western, ya wanna know why?"

"This oughta be good."

"Because the little mixed-raced chick is the one telling you to get the fuck outta town."

The sadism I'd seen lurking in the back of his orbs rushed to his pupils and whites. "You think you can get to that Colombia River in time, sweetheart? Huh, do ya?"

This was where I brought the humiliation part. I worked my face into a smile.

"But I thought we were just having a drink, you and me. You, looking like you just stepped off a movie set, and me, well—" I paused for theatrics. "Yet now you seem upset, almost rattled."

The flirtatious hottie was gone. The bully was here to protect the bruised ego. His breathing increased. He looked like he wanted to slap my face with the back of his hand. This was a man accustomed to being in control. I'd taken it from him. Not only could he not hit me in front of all these witnesses, he couldn't find words to put me in my place either.

I drew the moment out as far as I could until finally, I said, "And the answer is yes."

"Huh?" He asked.

"Yes, I can get to this blade in time. Besides, I imagine you normally have your lackeys do the dirty stuff."

He took a deep inhale. I moved my hand to Norma and unsnapped the hilt latch. His eyes flicked to the movement. Deep rouge flooded his eyes. The bully wanted out of the cage.

"All good here?" Tyler's deep voice boomed from behind Jesse Arlo. Without turning around, he told Tyler everything was peaches. He gave me a final smile, but it was as toothless as a newborn escargot's. In a quick move, he hopped off the bar stool and turned to face Tyler. At somewhere around 6'2", he looked up to Tyler.

"Think it through, buddy," Tyler said.

"I ain't like my boy you tossed earlier."

"Again, think it through, buddy."

He pushed past Tyler and headed for the door. Tyler followed closely at his heels. I exhaled and felt the room spinning. I pulled the thick wings of my hair back off my face and exhaled deeply. Lucy wiped the bar down in front of me. Then after drying her hands on her jeans she reached out and took both my hands in hers.

"Welcome to the Horse and Buggy, sweetheart," she said. She removed the Truly that I'd barely touched and replaced it with a clear liquid. A lime sat on the rim. She also poured herself one.

"Tequila?" I said.

"Yup, on me. Get it, girl."

"Okay, but just the one I'm driving," I said and knocked the drink back. It burned going down.

"Good girl." She smiled. "Lucy, like it says on the tag. And you are?"

"Chloe," I said. "Nice to meet you. And thanks for being so friggin' nice."

"It can be intimidating coming into a bar like this by yourself. We chicks gotta stick together."

"I won't argue that," I said.

"What're ya looking for, Chloe? I'm assuming you didn't come in here to meet charming individuals like those two douchebags, but you're here for some reason, so," she spread her arms wide. "How can I help?"

I told her just about everything I knew. I didn't feel that she was connected to the crew of guys at all, and she seemed, I don't know, trustworthy. And definitely savvy A.F.

"Based on what you've told me and the snippets I overheard, I'd have to agree with you. These assholes are obviously here for your sheriff, not some job like your deputy friend thinks. But hey, I'm just a bartender."

That was all I needed. I definitely had to get to Boulder and warn him. And then I'd stay out of it—let the paid professionals handle it. I felt a huge relief. I plunked the unused lime wedge into the shot glass and stepped off the bar stool.

"Lucy, you rock. Thank you."

"You be good, Chloe, and let the sheriff and his deputies handle this shit. I don't want to read about you in the *Valley Times*. Not that I read that shit," she laughed.

"Nobody does," I agreed.

Chapter Fifteen

I decided to blow off school on Wednesday. Like I said, I really didn't need to show up. There were basically four groups of seniors going to school at this point. Group one was the kids on the brink of passing or failing. They were the ones hustling like hell class to class. They'd rush red-faced, clutching books to chests and panting like Golden Retrievers chasing down Frisbees. The second group was more relaxed. They'd already done what was needed. They'd hang out just to socialize and make sure they all liked each other's social media pages.

Fake laughs. Big hugs. Endless promises of lasting friendships even though they might be going to different colleges. So annoying. Obnoxious are the needy. The next group was the majority. They were definitely going to graduate but needed decent attendance to do it. But the fourth group was me and the other unicorns. We had the grades and didn't need the perfect attendance record. In my case, the last thing I wanted to do was hang with the cool kids and mean girls. Most of which cower in fear of a future without one another. The needy truly are obnoxious.

Instead of school, I decided it was time to see Boulder and give him what I had regardless of the admonishment that would no doubt come. The greater good and all that, right? I figured once that's all done, I could go over my funds and plot my European adventure, cause come hell or high fucking water...

* * *

He tossed his stetson on his desk and leaned forward on his large hands. "You've been doing what? Didn't we just have a conversation about this?" The corners of the sheriff's eyes seemed to turn crimson.

"Raven, get the hell in here!" Sheriff Boulder bellowed.

The deputy came through the door un-phased by her boss's rage. She closed the door behind her and stood with hands behind her back. To look at her, she could have been three days into watching a golf tournament. She was cooler than a cucumber on ice.

"Matter of fact, don't close that door I want Steve in here as well."

Raven Tawanna reached backward and opened the door without taking her eyes off the sheriff. I realized in that moment she could probably back down a mother bear with her stare. Officer Burris entered and stood beside the deputy.

Steve Burris was a native Oregonian. He came to our sweet little town about three years ago. At twenty-nine with a square jaw, no facial hair, and light brown eyes, he was another member of law enforcement that my high school compatriot chicks found sexy. He and his wife Trudy were the perfect marriage by definition. Still, that didn't stop the hot mean girls at my school from taking runs at him. In fact, it was probably the reason half of them found him so sexy. A man in uniform, fully committed to his wife. How fucking twisted are those chicks?

Burris stiffened up his five foot eleven-inch posture, but it didn't help hide his anguish at what was coming.

"Did you two know what Chloe's been up to? Playing Nancy god damn Drew?"

"No, sir," Steve Burris said.

The sheriff moved his gaze to Raven.

"Sheriff Boulder neither—"

"Not now, Chloe," he said. "Let's have it, Tawanna."

"As a police officer, it's my duty to make myself accessible to the citizens of Bucksville. Chloe and I merely conferred as she's a concerned citizen of Bucksville."

"Cut the legal-speak Tawanna, we ain't in court."

The deputy moved to the wall and leaned against it. She slid a hand into her pocket and let her other arm hang at her side. "Come on, sheriff, these assholes in the 300 have people on edge. If Chloe has something to offer, I'm going to listen to her. Ignoring potential evidence wouldn't make sense."

The sheriff sat down heavily in his chair, causing it to creak beneath him. He lay his thick forearms on the desk and interlaced his fingers.

He looked out the window to his left a moment before speaking. I tried to get Raven's attention. I wanted to mouth the words 'I'm sorry.' I hope she didn't think I ratted her out. She knew what I was attempting and ignored me. I suppose I deserved it.

"Burris."

"Yes, sir."

"Scale of one to ten, how high are Tawanna and Chloe bullshitting me right now?"

Burris flicked his eyes at us but didn't turn his head from his boss. He cleared his throat, then fake coughed into his hand.

"Well, sir, I—"

"Save it, Burris. Chloe, do you have anything you want to say with all of us here before I decide whether to lock you up for, say, a couple of hours for being a pain in my ass?"

We all knew the sheriff would never do that. It was my cue to share.

"I was able to have a conversation with the number two guy. At least I think he's number two by the way he dresses like the number one guy—or boss, Jesse Arlo."

When cops meet your gaze with empty eyes, it's tough to tell if they want to lock you up or shoot you. I pressed on.

"He was drunk, so I thought, what a good time to get him to confess... something. Long story short, he said Sheriff Boulder was a bad boy in his past," I said. "Whatever that means."

"You spoke to this guy when he was drunk? Do you know how that could have turned out, Chloe?"

"Drunk asshole men? No, I can't say I've had any experience with that, Sheriff!" I laid on the sarcasm so thick a toddler would have clued in.

89

"Don't put any of that on me, Chloe."

When I relayed my conversation with the boss himself, Jesse Arlo, I thought for sure Boulder was going to lock me up. I kept telling myself his shouts of rage at me were based on his fear of me getting hurt. It was the only way to take it.

"Sheriff Boulder, if I may," Deputy Tawanna said, coming to my rescue.

"I think where Chloe's going with this is—" she stopped right there like we were riding in a car, and she slammed on the brakes. We waited. Rushing officer Tawanna would be useless.

"Initially I thought these guys were here to pull a job. And they still might be, but with this," she said, turning an upturned hand in my direction. "Maybe these guys are actually here for you, Jim. And seeing that they haven't stated their business, then you can expect a physical assault of some kind."

"I say we dig deeper on these assholes. Get all the intel we can. Maybe they've got warrants," Burris said. Boulder nodded. Burris left the room but didn't close the door behind him. Raven pushed off the wall and took a step forward.

"I'm going to keep looking at these guys, maybe even a little closer than before." she turned to me. "Thank you for your input. Now you're done. And, Sheriff, you need to look at photos and search that memory of—"

"I can help with that. I mean, I saw something. Then I promise I'll go." Before they could toss me out, I pulled out my phone.

"I checked out Arlo's Facebook page. Luckily his account's not private. Check out this photo." I handed my phone to officer Bad Ass. After a beat, she handed the phone to her boss. The photo was of Arlo and Carter. They stood shoulder to shoulder like a matched set with blazered arms folded across chests leaning against the 300's driver door. Both had identical sunglasses and two-dollar grins.

"Do you see how both guys have one ankle of their loafer crossed over the other?" I said.

"Uh-huh."

"Check out the number two dude. I'm betting that bulge at the ankle's not a gun but—"

"Ankle bracelet," Tawanna said. "I caught that."

Boulder raised his head and looked at me. I held out my hand for my phone. He handed it back and gave me a quick nod. We all know how many words a picture says. The sheriff's nod said the thousand words were all of approval. I wanted to breathe a sigh of relief but decided to do it outside. I put my phone away and tip-toed out the door as if navigating a minefield.

Chapter Sixteen

The fine members of the Bucksville sheriff's department were right. I've read hundreds of news stories where young people stick their nose where it doesn't belong, and the talking-news-head says, "It was a simple case of being at the wrong place at the wrong time, and now...the surviving family grieves."

It was time for me to butt out and get ready for Europe. I had As in Italian and Spanish. I wanted to be immersed in the languages and surrounded by the cultures. At least for a year or two, maybe more, who knows? Love ya, Bucksville, but I'm gone!

I floated through my shift at the laundromat as if on an Ambien trip. Was I professional and courteous to customers? Who can say. I was in another world. I spent my entire time researching European cities, food, lodging, Euro vs. dollar, flights, and everything else I could think of.

Near the end of the shift, I got a text from Shayna inviting me to coffee the next day to meet her girlfriend. So this was it. My bestie was going to introduce me to her betrothed. Would they marry one day, I wondered? I texted back I couldn't wait and polished it off with two happy face emojis, the rock and roll hand sign, and two hearts.

* * *

The Library is Buckville's newest gastropub and current *it* spot. Shayna said she'd try and get a table upstairs. The stair treads were thick dark wood, which appeared to float freely but were held in place by thick cables. The handrail was anchored to the ceiling by a set of cables, which gave the rail a similar free floating look. Once upstairs, I saw Shayna waiving from a small table in the back corner. From twenty feet away, Shayna's new gal was clearly a babe. Long auburn hair flowed to the middle of her back. Her athletic build also came with curves. They both stood as I neared.

"Hey girl," I said, giving Shayna a hug. Her girlfriend, who introduced herself as Lexi, waited with a kind smile. We hugged and introduced ourselves.

"Hey, we're in the same club," Lexi said.

"Oh, what club is that?" I asked.

She put a finger to her cheek. "Freckles," she said. "I hate mine, but yours are adorable."

"You're right. We are in the same club. I hate my freckles as well."

"You guys are so dumb," Shayna said. "They look great on both of you."

"So," Lexi said, "I heard you just found out about me and your gal here."

"Pretty much, yeah. But I gotta say whatever you're doing is working. Shayna's never looked this happy."

They turned to each other and did that giggly, scrunch up the face thing happy couples do. Twenty minutes later, we were into coffee refills and awaiting our order. The conversation was easy. I liked Lexi right off the bat. I was happy for Shayna. She not only seemed happy but relaxed. I can only imagine what it must feel like to live a life you wanted, not one society thought best for you.

"What?" Shayna asked.

"What?"

"I dunno, the way you're looking at us."

Lexi put a hand on Shayna's shoulder and moved close. "Can't you tell? She's happy for you. Happy you're happy. Am I right?"

"Dead on," I said.

Lexi kissed her on the cheek. I raised my coffee mug. "To you two. May your relationship endure and grow," I said. "Care for each other, and don't you bitches ever take yourselves too seriously."

"We can drink to that," they said as a chorus. We clinked coffee cups.

The three of us beamed like simpletons. If the smiles kept up another ten seconds, it would have become an uncomfortable moment. I almost said, 'Well that's done. What do we talk about now?' But we never got to the awkward moment because someone caught my eye. The Quiet One. He stood up three tables over from ours. He dropped a few bills on the table and made his way to the stairs.

"Fuck."

"What is it, Chlo?" Shayna asked.

"Mutha fu—is he stalking me?"

I was up out of my chair before having to explain to my lunch dates.

"Hey. Hey you," I called.

He shot me a quick glance, then moved down the stairs. He nearly knocked the waitress over as she ascended the opposite side of the staircase. He ignored her 'scuse you' comment and kept moving. I exercised care, making sure I didn't knock her over when we passed each other. I called again just as my target hauled the door open and lunged onto the sidewalk. He didn't so much as look back or slow his gate. I had to maneuver around a beefy tourist in a floral pattern shirt. I yanked the door open and checked up and down the sidewalk. Nothing.

Fucking ghost.

My heart danced in my chest. But this wasn't rage that normally comes easy to me. This was fear. With Momma's drunk boyfriends, I can ramp up the rage engine and head straight to violence.

With the Quiet One, it was different. He kept finding me. How did I not see him when I arrived at the restaurant? Was he there first? Did he know my patterns? A lucky guess, maybe? It was not only the unknown that freaked me out, it was him. He was quiet and owned rapid movements like a predator. But predators strike. What was this guy waiting for? Clearly, he was here for Boulder but was there more? Was *I*...the more?

My heart rate was returning to normal. I was still freaked out but was good enough to head back inside and field the questions that would surely come from Shayna. Our food had arrived by the time I got back. In between bites of my Asian chicken salad, I laid out the story for my lunch dates.

"You've gotta tell Boulder. Wait, I'm sure you've already done that," Shayna said. "What did he say?"

"I've been given the law enforcement 'stand down Nancy Drew' order."

"Figured as much," Shayna said.

"But this is different now, Chloe. The bastard is stalking you. I say go back to the sheriff and tell him he needs to, I dunno, pull the dude in for questioning or something," Lexi said.

She had a point. "Yeah, I don't know. I need to think about it," I said. "Look, thanks for listening, but can we change the subject?"

With reluctance, the girls respected my wish. With the conversation on to graduation and future plans, we hung around another half-hour before goodbye hugs went around.

"Lexi, I'm a fan. Team Lexi all the way. Take care of my girl, she's kinda useless on her own," I said.

"Will do," Lexi said with a giant smile. Shayna called me a bitch and punched me in the arm.

I realized with all of Momma's antics, high school, and the creepy intruders in town, this lunch was exactly what I needed. You can't put a price on friendship. Shayna's probably the only person I'll really miss in old Bucksville. Well, she and Sheriff Boulder, too, I guess…and officer Bad Ass.

Oh crap.

Chapter Seventeen

Up to this point, I've been relating stories of Momma's horrible and wretched boyfriends. I think it's time I give Momma some slack here. She doesn't always pick complete losers. Not all of her boyfriends were creepy pervs trying to get with me, twenty-four-seven. Some were actually decent guys. I'd even go so far as to say some were even nice. But I never gave even those guys a break. Not me. Maybe I was selfish, but I just wasn't interested. I missed my daddy. He's who I wanted around, not Mr. Friday night or Mr. Saturday morning.

I was just as rude and ruthless with the nice guys as I was with the bad. Looking back, I think I wanted to punish Momma. Maybe I didn't want her happy. I sure wasn't. Or maybe I just wanted a normal mom. Wait, okay, she was normal but she was drunk- normal, and that pissed me off. That's why I never gave any of those guys a chance. Good, bad, or in the middle. When Daddy died, me and Momma both got sad. Momma turned to drink, and I turned mean and honed knife skills. But I'm the kid, and she's the mom. Be a mom, damn it! Shit, I'm supposed to be giving Momma slack here. Oh well. That's me. Chloe Savannah. I explain but I don't apologize. When I'm out of the house she can take up with whoever she wants. Let's hope she settles on a nice guy. Either way, I won't give two shits because I'll be gone.

Momma was out when I got home. The house wasn't spit-shine clean anymore, but it wasn't three-day binge looking either. After doing my knife throws I grabbed one of my carvings and post-up on the front stoop. The piece would be about eighteen inches long when I was done. I was carving yet another totem pole. This one had three different women's faces bookended by ravens top and bottom. It was a real bear of a project, but nothing good comes easy, right?

I've had the carving of the women's faces and passerine birds done for quite some time, but the difficulty is manipulating emotion and expression into the wooden faces. These women were tougher than leather, and I wanted it to show the confidence in their countenances. I didn't want to be left with their faces appearing wooden—pun totally intended.

I was at it an hour before Momma came home. Her smile read that although there was a little liquor to it, she genuinely adored her daughter. A hint of water gathered at the corners of her eyes, and I'd be lying if I didn't say it hit me like a punch to the gut. In my mind, I was six thousand miles away, strolling Italy's cobblestone streets. But dead-on in front of me was my mother. A woman who loved me with all her heart, even the broken parts. How in god's name could I take off and follow my dreams? Family is what matters no matter where in the deck of cards they're drawn from. I felt a guilty pang of selfishness that pierced like the tip of one of my blades.

"You're home," she said. She hugged me tight and kissed me on the cheek.

"Okay, Momma, okay," I said and peeled away. "Are you hungry? I think we've got enough for a decent stir fry."

"I'd prize nothing more highly than to have dinner with my love...lovely daughter."

I've always felt that drunks come across more drunk when they try and hide their drunkenness. Momma tried to refuse the help I offered her up the steps, but I knew deep down she appreciated it.

We were low on grub, but I managed to turn the beef strips, broccoli, yellow carrots, soy, and ginger powder into a half-decent meal. For Momma, it was a gourmet meal because, as you can imagine, Joselyn can be a bit of a meal skipper. After dinner, she did an arms overhead, full-body stretch. What a shame, I thought. Her body was still toned with curves in the right places. My god, it pained me to think of the countless sweaty losers she lets have at that fine body. The thought made me shiver.

"Whatsa matter, baby? Ya cold?"

"No, Momma just—"

And that's when I ruined one of the few pleasant evenings we spent together.

"I'm leaving, Momma. Right after school. I've got money saved, and a plan all mapped out."

Momma looked at me as if some of the words came at her in Japanese. Her lashes fluttered beneath her creased brow. Her mouth turned downward.

"You're..you're leaving me?"

My god, she sounds like an effing toddler.

"Not you. And not forever...or maybe I don't know. I just...I mean Buckville is—this town ain't me, Momma. Tell me that comes as no surprise."

"Have I done something to you?" She sat-fell down on the couch as if my words had pushed her there. I imagine my eyes popped to the size of pancakes. Her eyes fluttered as she held up a palm to me.

"Okay, all right. I know my drinking can at times—"

A truck rumbled up to the house and skidded to a stop. We both looked at each other questioningly. Momma shrugged her shoulders. I hurried to the window and flipped the shade. A beat up red and white Ford F-150 shut down. Headlights went dark. What stepped out, and I mean what, was much taller than the truck's roof and wider than a city bus. Long hair fell from his melon sized head onto massive shoulders.

He slammed the door and stood beside the truck, and stared at the house. He had the same kind of sway that Momma usually had. His thick wool shirt hung like a tent. The waist size of his jeans was way north of fifty. Momma came and stood beside me. She had the good sense to keep quiet. I questioned her with my eyes—the same shrug of the shoulders.

You just don't remember, is all.

"Hello in there. I'm looking for two young ladies. A mom and daughter team. Both hot." He found his question amusing.

His voice boomed like he was two people. I noticed the blinds were shaking, then realized it was my grip on them. I didn't have to look at Momma to know she was scared shitless too.

"What the hell have you done, Joselyn?" I whispered.

"Nothin'. I've never seen that big son of a bitch before. I swear."

And that was just it. The guy had never been in our house, he's not the size asshole anybody'd forget. But no telling if Momma flirted with him in some bar, or god knows what out behind the bar. Yuk!

"Look, ladies, I know you're in there, so no point shuttin' off lights of hiding under beds cause I'm comin' in."

He rolled his massive head side to side. It was theatrical, but I could have sworn I heard his neck bones cracking from our living room. Momma wrapped a hand around my bicep and squeezed. She shook like it was twenty below.

"Whoops, where are my manners? My name's Josh Teagan. Ya'll know my brother Brett. I believe he banged the older one and got a knife to the throat from the little firecracker daughter."

His laugh dripped with sadistic intent. I could rush out the front door, juke left, and be gone, but Momma would be a sitting duck. And I'd never get help in time. Momma squeezed my arm hard. I eased my hand down to Norma's hilt but didn't really feel all that confident.

He rolled his neck again—a man gearing up to do bad. He pushed off the truck and came at the house. When he hit the first step, the entire house shook from roof shingles to foundation.

I grabbed Momma's face in both hands. "Momma, baseball bat under the couch. Stand on that side of the door." To her credit, she went straight into action as if we'd rehearsed it. I took up a spot on the other side. Norma Jean's leather handle nestled into my sweaty palm.

"When that grizzly bear motherfucker comes through, you swing with everything you got. Don't hesitate. I'll be coming from—"

I never got the words out. The front door flew into the house. His kick blew the top hinge right off, causing the top of the door to swing in and catch me. I partially blocked it, but it made my arm smack into my head. I staggered back. Momma kept her nerve. Her two-handed swing looked as good as any man's. The problem was the grizzly bear expected us to defend ourselves. He took the bat full on the forearm but didn't groan, grimace, or even wince. The only sound was his mocking laughter. Momma loaded up again, but he caught the bat and tossed it aside like it was a nuisance of a chopstick.

I'd gathered myself and came in fast with a couple of feints. He got into a defensive position. He moved well for a big man and tracked my blade with a calm that was more than a little unsettling. I sliced his forearm. Blood trickled down, but all he did was grin.

"This is fun, ain't it? Little brother said y'all was fun."

Momma grabbed a vase and smashed it over the back of his head. She had to leap in the air just to get the vase to the height of his giant melon. I hated that vase and was glad it shattered but was disheartened when the man reacted like a fly landed on him. He spun and backhanded Momma. She sailed over the coffee table and onto the couch. She lay motionless. His attention was back to me, but I was already on him. My blade sunk into his side above the hip bone. He wore a bewildered expression like the comic book movie villain who thinks he's impenetrable until the bullet pierces his flesh.

Momma was still out. The house, for all the commotion, was silent other than our heavy breathing. He put his hand over mine. I tried to jerk free, but my hand was in a vice. I twisted, hoping the cut would become fatal.

Yeah, you wish, Chloe.

He yanked the knife out. My hand was hidden in his. His eyes locked on my wrist. He was going to break it for sure. I put everything I had into the knee to his nuts, but he must have had layers of fat for protection. He barely flinched. He grabbed the side of my head like it was a golf ball and slammed it into the cupboard. Bright sparks spread in front of me. My legs gave out, but he kept me from slumping to the ground. I was lifted off the floor and tossed into the cupboards over the sink. I hit the cheap pressboard, fell to the sink, bounced off, and hit the floor hard. I could hear, but I couldn't see a thing.

His footsteps sounded like hundred-pound kettlebells tumbling through our little house. Light began peeking through the dark wall in front of my eyes. I heard popping sounds. I got to my knees and threw up. I smelled gun powder. Shots. Shots being fired. What the hell? Heavy boots retreated down the hall. My vision came nearly all the way back. Momma was having a tough time getting up from the couch. A pair of survivors is what we were. I screamed for her to stay down, but no sound came from my lips. I crawled on hands and knees toward the shots—not smart, I know. But the hint of perfume that pierced the gun powder was undeniable. Deputy Tawanna was in my house. She was firing from the hall into the massive man who stalked forward like a zombie, yet was very much alive.

The deputy's clip would be empty any second. Not that I was counting. I reached into my front pocket and hauled out The Girl, my back up Bowie knife. I caught up to the big asshole and sliced deep into the Achilles. He cried out this time.

He looked down at me and said, "Son of a—"

I took the knife and plunged it as far into the calf muscle as I could. Two more shots boomed in the house. I had nothing left. I didn't have the strength to crawl or roll out of the way. I just covered up in the fetal position and braced for the four hundred-pound tree to fall on me. If it hurt, I don't remember.

When I came to, Tawanna and Momma were sitting on the couch panting like they'd been holding their breath under water.

"She's back," Raven said calmly.

"Oh, my baby!" Momma said and ran to me.

"Okay, Momma. I'm okay, you're smothering me, though. Momma!"

Momma cried and kept on crying. The deputy had Boulder on her cell. He was inbound along with the coroner, EMT, and whoever else showed up for parties like these. As I cleaned my blades, I stared into nothing. Nothing except countries far from here…with me in 'em.

Momma was too messed up to relay our one-act play with the giant, so I did all the talking. Sheriff Boulder didn't even attempt to control his rage. He mostly paced and said 'god dammit' every ten seconds, so I was pretty much talking with Raven, who wrote everything down.

"Why do you call your backup knife The Girl?" Raven asked.

"Marilyn Monroe's character in The Seven Year Itch. The Girl. Just…The Girl."

The deputy didn't write that down. I couldn't tell if my blade's name moved her one way or another. The sheriff's boot stomps were nearly as booming as the giant's had been. Men stomp, I suppose. Some men are good, and some evil, like giant Josh Teagan who lay dead in my hallway. I felt a hysterical laugh coming on, but it was quashed by a wave of nausea. I ran and puked into the kitchen sink. Happily, there weren't any dishes in there.

After rinsing my mouth, I asked Raven how she happened along in the nick of time.

"Bartender at Grady's Bar called and said some giant white man was bragging about what he was about to do. The threat seemed credible. You know the rest."

"Well, Momma and I are so fucking thank—"

"Just doing my job, Chloe," she said. She went and joined the others with the big project ahead of them.

The big man was too big for the cart-away stretcher. The paramedics stood scratching heads while the sheriff and deputy pondered. I couldn't sit idle.

"Hang on," I said.

I went to my bedroom and pulled thirty-five feet of braided rope from under my bed. I asked Boulder and Tawanna to partially roll the giant over. I looped rope under his arm, then back behind his head, then under and around the other shoulder.

"Just pull him to the kitchen and stop there. I have a plan," I said.

Tawanna caught on right away. She, Boulder, and one of the paramedics cinched the rope around his forearms and held tight with their hands. With a coordinated effort, they hauled the giant man down the narrow hallway. They were huffing and puffing by the time they reached the kitchen.

I was already out the door. I hopped in my truck and backed it up to the bottom step. The group, including Momma, watched me as if I were a magician in the middle of a trick. I took up the excess rope and took it to my truck. I tied a simple Farmer's Loop Knot around my trailer hitch. Everyone clued in to the plan by this time. I hopped back into my truck. Boulder and Tawanna together slid chairs aside, creating a clear path.

I eased the accelerator pedal down and rolled forward. The rope became taught. The truck groaned a moment. I gave it a little more gas. The corpse slid along the living room floor toward the door. I could only imagine the paramedics' relief. I stopped when the body reached the doorway.

Boulder and the deputy knelt down and turned the man on his side. Boulder gave me the nod. I eased forward. The giant barely fit through the door. His head hit every step on the way down…but what did he care?

The paramedics applauded me with grins on their faces.

"It ain't over yet, fellas," I said. "Now you've got to find a way to get him into the bus."

Their smiles disappeared. I untied the rope, parked my truck, and went back inside. The next part wasn't my problem.

When the cavalry finally cleared out, I ignored Momma's tearful apology and headed for a shower. I reeked of sweat, fear, blood, and vomit. I hurt like hell. I was uber pissed at Momma but too sore to give her grief. She brought this shit to the door—*through* the fucking door. However, there was a slight pain in the side of my gut, and that was pity. I truly felt sorry for Momma.

I turned the heat as hot as it would go and climbed under. It was the first time I showered with five knives within reach. I was unsure if I'd be able to sleep that night. One challenge at a time. For now, it was time to scrub the behemoth's DNA and everything else off my aching body.

Seriously?

Chapter Eighteen

I'd never had a hangover before. You probably think it's because, shit, obviously Chloe doesn't drink but one or two drinks in a sitting. That's true to a point. I've had a beer here and a wine cooler there. Momma is a mess so I don't usually drink to excess. But I wasn't going to abstain altogether because, in my twisted brain, that would mean Momma took that from me along with my shot at a regular life. If I seem like a risk-taker, I don't think so. Because if alcoholism is hereditary, then I might be all right. You see Momma's drinking was brought on by depression—the loss of Daddy. Neither her nor Daddy came from a long line of drinkers. Just a theory, and I could care less if it's accurate or not.

Regardless, the day after the impromptu shit kicking party with the giant, I felt like what I can imagine a nasty hangover feels like.

I put my head in both hands and psyched myself into crawling out of bed. Three Advil and a gallon of water was job number one. Once my feet hit the floor, it seemed to take an hour to get to the kitchen cabinet with the headache pills. I ran the water as cold as it would go. Hmm, hot water for the body and cold water for thirst. I was pouring my second glass when Momma called out from her room. I put the glass down and went to check on her.

"How're you feeling, baby?"

"Fine, Momma. No wait, I feel like a motor home ran me over...twice," I said.

She smiled a moment. Then tears came.

"Not now, Momma, please. Are you hungry?"

"Are you really leaving me, Chlo?"

I was flabbergasted. "What? Is that really what you're asking right now? Oh, how completely priceless. We were attacked by a fucking Sasquatch last night—your fault by the way, and you want to know—you just want to know if I'll still be here to look after your drunk ass. We could have died last night, Joselyn. Is that why you want me here? To die along with you when the next mountain comes through that door? Cause you can bet he's coming, the way you live your life!"

I rushed to her bedside and pointed at her. "You are so goddamn selfish. I'll clean up your mess, do your laundry and make your meals, but I won't sit here and get beaten to death because of the company you keep. Got it? Fuck!" I was all-out screaming.

Momma cried and said something I couldn't comprehend.

"What? What are you—are you slurring? Did you have a drink already?"

Her body began to shake slightly as if an electrical charge caused a tremor to rip through her. Her arms lay at her sides. She lifted a frail hand and pointed to something on the comforter.

"What? Just tell me what you want. Another blanket?"

"I can...clee...can't fall...fall...feel my arms. I...thee...sh...shh...arrma...ma."

"Oh, shit, Momma," I said and peeled back the covers. "Try again. Can you move them?"

Tears rushed down her face. I knew she was trying. She looked terrified. I probably had tears in my eyes. I don't remember. I hustled out of her room and grabbed my cell—punched in the three numbers.

"Yes, this is Chloe Savannah. I think my mother's having a stroke, or—please send an ambulance. Huh? What?" I quickly gave my address. "They know the house, trust me."

Momma was rushed to the hospital, and sure enough, she had somewhere between a mini and full stroke. I was nearly paralyzed with fear. I should have balled my eyes out but as usual, rage burned inside and threatened to ooze out my skin. I was pissed at life—pissed at God too if he was up there. I slouched in the uncomfortable chair like a teenage boy—legs spread, the whole bit. I couldn't have given a shit it wasn't ladylike. I was done, spent, pissed, totally tapped out. If not for the fact that the doctor who came to update me was my G.P., I'd have stayed seated.

"Doctor Griffiths, hi," I said and gave her a brief hug. My voice was hoarse. I couldn't remember how long since my last appointment but I was pretty sure she wasn't nearly as gray haired the last time we met.

"What's the—is she?"

"She's in pretty good shape. A little paralysis on her right arm, but there's a good chance she'll gain full use, or close to it. Her legs are fine, fully functioning. Her speech is slow but not slurry like you described when the stroke occurred."

"I read on the internet that—"

"You should stay off that thing, Chloe."

"—that her alcoholism makes her like, what a, candidate, or more prone to have a stroke if—"

And from out of nowhere, I had no words, only tears. I felt my head being pulled into my doctor's breast. Her soothing words seemed to make it worse, but I wasn't ready to pull away. I cried. Cried hard.

Through tears and nose running like a faucet, I told my doctor we'd been fighting and that the stroke was my fault. Doctor Griffiths eased me off of her.

"Stop it, Chloe. You stop that nonsense right now."

I felt like I was five years old.

"Your Joselyn has been unhealthy for a very long time. Something like this was one of many possible outcomes that can and could have happened. Do you hear me, young lady?"

I nodded but wasn't completely sold.

"Good. Now, your mother's going to be a guest here for a few days, so we can keep an eye on her. We also need to determine what level of physiotherapy will be necessary."

She put a gentle hand under my chin. "Are we good as we can be right now?"

"Yes, ma'am."

"It's Carol or doctor Griffiths, young lady," she said with a sympathetic smile. "Would you like to see her?"

**

I was sick with nerves. I had no idea what to say to Momma. I didn't have any words. None. I was granted a reprieve when I saw she was asleep when I entered. I sat in another uncomfortable hospital chair and watched her sleep. She looked peaceful—peaceful and smaller than I remembered, yet I'd seen her just hours ago. After ten minutes, I dragged myself up and left the room.

I felt like I was adrift in a row boat watching both oars gently floating away with the current. I knew what I needed. I hoped my bestie would come through.

"Hey Shayna, can I ask a huge favor?"

"Aw, Chloe, I'm so sorry about Momma, I just heard," she said.

Small towns for ya.

"Ask away. Anything."

"Do you think—do you think I could borrow Rusty? Take him for a ride?"

"You don't even have to ask," she said. "And you can take him out anytime?"

"Thanks, Shayna."

"Do you want company, or is this a solo ride?"

"God luv ya Shay, but I think I'd like to just—"

"Totally, totally get it. See you in, what, fifteen?"

"Sounds about right?"

"We'll be out front, you don't even need to come down to the stables."

When I pulled up to Shayna's sprawling mansion, Rusty was saddled and ready to go as promised. Shayna held onto the bridle in one hand and waved with her other. Rusty started bobbing his head up and down, playfully beating his hoof on the flagstone before I even got out of the truck. I always thought it was like a dog wagging its tail.

"Hey, girl," Shayna said. She gave me a big squeeze. Her eyebrows formed a sympathetic arch. "How's Momma?"

"She'll be all right, I guess. She's in good hands, anyway."

I stroked Rusty along his forehead and nose. He was raring to go. Shayna and I were quiet a moment. The warm breeze blew our hair around our faces. We'd known each other so long that silences weren't uncomfortable for us. Shayna would probably have waited all day in that moment for me to either speak or mount up and go. Because it was her I didn't feel rushed. After a few more strokes and a heavy sigh.

"If she keeps living the way she does, she won't be with us long, Shay." I held Rusty's eye when I said it. I couldn't look at Shayna in that moment. History and the science of medicine said I'd be saying goodbye to Momma sooner than later. I snorted the way Rusty does as if that would keep my tears at bay. Finally, I met Shayna's gaze.

She had tears in her eyes. My eyes began to fill. She hugged me again because that's what normal people do in a fucked up abnormal world. I pulled out of the embrace for fear of oncoming body shaking sobs and hopped onto the gorgeous thoroughbred.

With an easy grip on the reins, I looked down at my longtime friend. With a slender hand, she blocked the sun's rays. I asked, "How's your girl Lexi? Y'all still in that sickening honeymoon stage?"

"Oh hell yeah," We both laughed, and not because it was funny.

"I shouldn't be more than an hour."

"Okay, Chlo. Any longer, call me, or I'm coming to look for you."

* * *

Shayna's property is just under ten acres. The first half-mile in any direction from the mansion is wide open flat land before you get to any trails and forest of any kind. I couldn't have held Rusty back if I tried. We both wanted the same thing anyway. He took off like a shot the minute I steered him away from Shayna. I put my boots to his ribs in a gentle but racing way, and we bolted. Shayna's wolf howl followed us until the wind and distance killed the sound.

Rusty galloped like he was back on the track and first out of the gate. I'm certainly a few pounds heavier than the jockeys that rode him in his younger days but it didn't seem to bother him. We accelerated to the first stand of mini sequoias like it was the finish line. Rusty leaped onto the trail like he needed to win by more than a nose. The trail banked left almost immediately. I leaned at the right time, and I think Rusty knew I would. We trusted each other. If a horse doesn't trust you or senses a lack of confidence, it can be a disaster.

"Come on, boy, let's see what you've got left in the tank."

My adrenalin spiked. I wanted to ride my problems away. But I was also nervous-excited because I've always been a good rider but I hadn't ridden nearly as much as in my younger days. Riding a horse is not like riding a bike as far as time away. Bikes are a mechanical thing. A horse is a twelve hundred-pound mammal with a personality or in this case, a horsenality. Sure, riding will come back to you, but there are like a thousand more variables, and this ain't no bicycle.

The first mile of the trail is wide and well worn. And also not too serpentine, so we moved through at a good clip. After that, the trail narrows and has more ups, downs, and sharp turns. Rusty slowed pretty much on his own. Eventually, we slowed to a nice canter. Rusty breathed harder than in the old days. I suppose I was too. We're both older and a little heavier so, whatever. Still, we were both out doing what we love.

I envisioned riding horses on the Italian and Spanish countrysides and beaches as well. Why not? My grin was ear to frigging ear until I thought about Momma, laid up in a hospital bed. Daddy's suicide is what started killing her, but the booze is what will end her life before her projected expiry date. I chuckled to myself for reasons I couldn't figure. I suppose Momma and I should consider ourselves lucky after surviving a human grizzly bear attack…but not so much. Momma would be gone soon, and for me, life after Momma would look like a ton of therapy, which I'm sure I'd never indulge in. So…

Shut up and enjoy the ride, you idiot. Don't be so extra!

Chapter Nineteen

"How was the ride?"

"Exactly what I needed, Shayna, thanks." We hugged. "I don't think Rusty wanted to come back."

"I appreciate you running him like you do. He misses the track something serious," she smiled.

"He's a good boy."

"To you, he is." She laughed.

"Thanks again and—"

"I don't know what life is going to look like for Momma, Chloe, but I'll be here for her."

"What do you mean?"

"I know you, Chloe, and I know what you need."

I let her get it out.

"You need to go. Like Rusty needed the racetrack, you need to fly, anywhere but Bucksville. This town is choking you."

"But—"

"I'm trying to tell you Momma will be taken care of. We'll be here for her. Like I said, I know you. You're restless. You need to roam. It's written all over your cute freckled face and has been since the sixth grade. Before that even."

"It sounds like you're giving me permission, which is really sweet but I could never put that on you."

"Us, me and my parents. I know my parents would do whatever is needed."

I was stunned.

"I know this is coming out of left field, and I'm not telling you what to do, I'm just saying if you want to go...you can. I have your back."

At first, anger boiled inside me. Who was she to know my business and grant me...but then I realized that Shayna's offer was the kindest gesture a friend could ever offer. It was above and beyond. I wrapped my arms around her.

"You're so fucking sweet," I said.

I could never put my mother's responsibility in my best friend's hands. Not in a million years and told her so. I'd give Momma whatever care she needed once doctor Griffiths clued me in and then I'd be on my way. If Shayna wanted to check in from time to time, then so be it. But no way would I allow her to be Momma's full-time caregiver.

I climbed into my truck and as I sat there we spoke for another ten minutes. I told her of my European plans, and she lit up.

"I fucking love that plan. My god, you can use your Spanish and Italian—oh this is awesome." She pointed a finger at me. "I told you, you need to fly."

"Yeah, you know me well," I said. "Will you and Lexi come visit once I'm set up?"

"Try and stop us...sis," she said. Sis. We'd always been like sisters and now it felt as though my sister had been returned.

I turned the engine over. I drove around the roundabout and watched her in my rearview once I was on the straightaway.

I'm seriously going to miss that girl.

* * *

The ride with Rusty and the sweet gesture from Shayna really recharged my battery. I swung back by the hospital to check on Momma.

"You're awake," I said. I walked to her and grabbed her hand.

"Hey, baby," she said. Her voice was weak and croaky. Her lids seemed heavy but she was still able to put a smile to her eyes.

"How do you feel?"

"Tired." She blinked slowly. "Did Doctor Griffiths fill you in?"

111

"She did, although I'm waiting to hear what sort of physio you'll need."
She barely managed a nod.

"I'm going to be here a couple days, it looks like."

"That's good. You get some rest, that's the main thing," I said.

"Okay, thanks for…coming. Thanks…" She dozed off.

I went out to reception and asked for Doctor Griffiths. She was paged and showed up ten minutes later. I was told that Momma would receive a full work-up of tests then they'd let me know what her immediate future would look like.

"The good news is there's no paralysis, but she does have some hemiparesis on her right side."

"Hemi—"

"Some weakness. She's probably looking at three to five months of physio, weekly at first, and then the visits will taper off. Again, this is a guesstimate. We'll know a lot more after some tests."

My mind went straight to the medical insurance side of the ledger. This was going to take some creative mathematics. The doctor put her hands on my shoulders.

"I know that look. Insurance, right?"

I didn't answer. I just stared into the doctor's hazel-colored eyes.

"We've got options, don't worry. I'll email you some material. Your mother is going to be fine."

"Not if she keeps up—"

"Never mind that. It's not going to help to go there. One thing at a time, okay, Chloe?"

I nodded, feeling small. Incredibly small. When doctor Griffiths let go of my shoulders, I thanked her and moved toward the exit. I moved my hand to the hilt of Norma Jean but she wasn't there. I'd left her in my truck figuring the hospital might have had a metal detector. Back in the truck I pulled Norma from under the driver's seat and stroked the blade before putting her back in the scabbard. As pathetic as it is, Norma's my security blanket. Some people need emotional support dogs, I need Norma Jean. To each her own.

* * *

I needed to do something. I could have gone home and cleaned house but crazy as it sounds it would be too lonely without Momma. I could crank up some music and go to town on just about any room but that wouldn't cut it. Even though Momma was very much alive, the house would feel as though she'd passed.

I went back to Sheriff Boulder and his situation. After a quick little ponder, I decided I'd head back to the Horse and Buggy. What could a little more surveillance hurt? That was the plan until I stepped out of my house and saw Kyle walking toward my door. I had to blink twice. He'd never been to my place before—had never been invited. It totally threw me off. It didn't help my stultification any that he looked so damn hot. He wore skinny jeans but not too skinny. His plain white t-shirt put his lean fitness on full display. The shirt hung loose but a portion was tucked into the front of his belt buckle. I don't normally like surprises, but dang...

His thick bangs fell down over his forehead. And there was just enough product in it to make it look like he'd just woken up.

"I went by the hospital but missed you. I hope you don't mind me showing up like this."

His mild discomfort added to his hotness. What was it about this guy?

"Not at all. Thanks for checking on me. That is what you're doing right?"

"Yeah, ah totally. I was worried when I heard about Joselyn. Is she gonna be all right?" He asked, slowly closing the distance between us.

"Some rehab work in the future, but yeah, I guess she'll be fine."

"Your doctor wouldn't tell me much seeing as I'm not family," he said.

"You know that's really sweet that you went there."

"Aw, come on. I care about you, Chloe. I think you know that."

His foot rested on the bottom step. He leaned against the handrail and smiled. My knees nearly buckled. With all that had been going on, I hadn't taken any time for me. And now this hottie was here...for me. I despise the word horny, it's such a dude's term but that was the word on my mind, and the feeling coursing through my every cell. We both knew we had the house to ourselves and we'd been playing cat and mouse for so dang long.

I'd had sex one time, and it was awful. I wasn't really into the guy, and he wouldn't shut up about how hot I was. It was so effing annoying. I couldn't wait for him to roll off me. But this already felt different. I wanted Kyle and wanted him right then.

"Wanna come in? The place is a mess, but—"

"Sure," he said.

I kept the tour quick, which wasn't a stretch. He complimented as best he could. To his credit, there really isn't much to work with on our house. Kyle's parents were rich. Not like Shayna's parents but definitely upper, upper-middle class. I could have felt self-conscious about having him in my home but being around him was so easy, I didn't care. Besides, I had other things on my mind.

He moved slowly around my room, picking up carvings and overwhelming me with compliments about my work. A lap of my bedroom doesn't take long. Pretty soon he ran out of real estate and carvings and we found ourselves face to face beside my bed. He had a light soap smell—my favorite. I couldn't take it anymore. I stepped in and kissed him. He kissed me back. His mouth was warm—perfectly warm. Our tongues danced. His kiss was the perfect mix of hard yet soft—whatever that means. We eased onto my bed. I opened my legs. His body moved into the space. With clothes still on, our pelvises pushed against each other's. The kissing got more intense. What a send off this would be before my trip. Kyle was the only thing on my mind. I was totally focused on him.

He ran his hands over my breasts. I grabbed his ass and pulled him closer. He sat up. I helped him off with his shirt.

My god, those abs!

I quickly cheated a look at the muscle at the hip that dives to the pelvis—my favorite muscle. Water polo had really chiseled this guy. I took my sweater off. We kissed some more.

"I have a condom," he whispered.

"Yes," I said back breathlessly.

We each worked at our own belts. Pants slid down legs and were kicked

114

off the bed. We met panty to boxer briefs a moment before he reached down to his jeans. I thought I was going to explode as he fumbled with the condom. Finally, I helped him.

"That's it," he said. "We got it."

He climbed back on top of me. I was ready. More than ready. He suddenly looked worried. Shyness, I thought. His body shivered a moment, and then...

"Shit, aw shit. No! I'm so sorry," he said with a final shiver.

"What is it?" I said, sitting up.

"I...I came. You're just so fucking hot," he said.

The condom snapped off with a rubber band sound. He tossed it onto his jeans and lay back with a hand over his eyes.

"It's okay, Kyle. It happens," I said, not knowing really what to say.

I'd love to tell you that for the next ten minutes, Kyle and I hugged, kissed, and laughed like long-time lovers, then shared a beautiful full-length round two. But the opposite happened.

"I gotta go."

"What? Why? Let's just hang out, fool around, and we'll go again," I said.

"Sorry," he said, sliding a pant leg up his leg.

"Sorry? That's it? Come on, Kyle," I said and grabbed him at the wrist. He pulled away like I was a leper.

"Whoa, take it easy."

"Look, this has never happened before, okay, so I'm out."

"Yeah, you said it's cause I'm hot," I said, trying to keep things light.

"Whatever."

"Whatever? You get me all worked up, and I get a whatever?"

"Yeah, I guess. See ya 'round," he mumbled.

"No, you won't," I said, going to the Chloe zone. "Now, get the fuck out of my house."

A look flashed through his eyes, then it was gone. I took it to be an 'arrogant jock' look, but I wasn't positive. It felt like a little darkness was in there.

European adventure here I come!

Chapter Twenty

I'm not going to bother mentioning how many knife throws I did after my non-romp with Kyle. By now, you know how short my fuse can run. In short, I punished every stump, post, and target I have set up outside my house. Norma Jean and The Girl did so much damage that a hand full of targets will need to be replaced.

A little over three months ago, I was on my way home from school, traversing my usual route. I made my usual stop at Saul's and once again inhaled the fragrant aromas of his bakery but purchased nothing. The songbirds accompanied me with their orchestral song on the last leg of my walk.

Twenty yards from home, I noticed some sort of animal activity on the hood of my truck, which was parked about twenty feet from the house. I slowed my pace and focused my gaze. A sharp-shined hawk was feasting on a pigeon. Right there, smack dab in the middle of my hood. It was amazing. Majestic.

The hawk picked up my presence and did a quick swivel of his head. He paused his meal and put an eye on me. I stopped in my tracks. With incredible slowness, I lowered myself to the ground and sat cross-legged. I slowed my breathing and observed. I hoped he didn't feel I was a threat. He kept his eye on me for what seemed like a full minute before returning to the kill. With each subsequent bite, his little head would pop up for a quick check on the frizzy-haired girl watching him.

We remained like that for at least five whole minutes before rumblings could be heard from inside my house.

Shit, Momma's up.

Great, my beautiful experience with nature was about to be ruined, and this poor little guy wasn't going to get to finish his meal. This was my thinking at the time. But to Momma's credit, she came out onto the porch and spotted the event immediately. She froze in place and, with a surgeon's care, eased the screen door closed behind her. She was now under the hawk's eye. She played it just as I had and stayed in one spot.

Eventually, she gained the raptor's trust, and he went back at the pigeon. Momma's and my eyes locked across the scene briefly. So much was said in that moment. We were at times worlds apart, but what we witnessed was remarkable. A shared experience we both appreciated. Nature was simple. Maybe we were supposed to live simply. This was where my thinking was, and Momma's gentle smile told me she was thinking the same thing.

The hawk kept at his prey for another fifteen minutes. Neither Momma nor I moved an inch and barely let ourselves blink for fear of missing even a second of the gift before us. The hawk raised its head, took a little turd on my truck, and then took flight with the scarce remains of the meal in his left talon. It was a good two minutes before either Momma or I moved or spoke to each other. I suspect neither one of us wanted that peaceful moment to end. Our shared calm before the inevitable tempest destined to return.

When I finally went in the house, we exchanged details of our day. We didn't dare spoil the experience by going at each other, nor did we need to talk about how amazing the spectacle was. Pleasantries done, we politely adjourned to our lairs. I immediately grabbed a carving stump and The Girl and busied myself with a carving.

It took me near all of those three months to complete the carving. It's about eight inches long made from a chunk of Tecate Cypress. It's of a hawk standing on a dead pigeon beneath its talon. As my laptop booted it up, I applied a thin coat of light brown paint to the hawk's wings, blew on it a few times, then set the piece aside.

Sitting crossed-legged on my bed with the laptop open, I began looking into Sheriff Boulder's past. He and his office probably had all the background they needed on Jesse Arlo, but I thought I'd look at the sheriff, particularly at his days with the California Highway Patrol. I figured there'd be plenty of information, being that he'd been a public servant.

I wanted to find the connection between Boulder and Arlo. I had to do something because sitting on my ass waiting for the deputy to call was not going to cut it. I went to the C.H.P. website and thought I might find a tab and enter his name there. Scrolling down, I came upon the significance of the badge and what each point of the star represents. Honor. Courtesy. Integrity. Knowledge. Judgment. Loyalty. Character. All seven points were held up by Bucksville's sheriff, in my opinion. Jim was a shining example.

Unable to find a tab to enter his name, I opened another search window and entered his name, C.H.P., and slowly typed the word crimes. Which felt intrusive. Four unrelated items down, I found "officer involved shooting." I had no choice but to click.

Three mini boxes from L.A. news sources covered the story. I clicked on the first one with the intent to skim the article. Officer James Henry Boulder was involved in a shooting during a routine traffic stop on the 405 Freeway. A woman was involved. Boulder was shot at, and...

That was enough for me. I scrolled down to a large white 'play' arrow of a Youtube video. I uncrossed my legs and lay on my stomach, and hit play. The video was shot from the police unit's vehicle's dash cam. Boulder's car parked a good fifteen yards behind an older silver Toyota Tercel. The camera shifted slightly before Boulder's back and shoulder came into view. He moved alongside the Freeway's solid concrete wall on the passenger side of the vehicle.

I couldn't see his face, but he was at least fifteen pounds lighter and moved more easily than he does today. The driver, a woman, was forced to lean across her passenger seat to roll the mechanical window down. They had words. Both vehicles rocked slightly as semis and large SUVs sped past. Boulder began making hand gestures as he spoke as if the woman either didn't understand what he was saying or maybe arguing with the C.H.P. officer.

Two minutes and forty seconds ticked by on the dash cam clock. Boulder continued to move his hands around. Eventually, the woman handed something to Boulder.

Long ass time to produce a D.L. lady.

Boulder moved back toward his vehicle with purpose. He crossed the camera's view. He suddenly ducked his head and shoulders as if he heard a loud noise from above. He turned toward the Tercel. His body jerked to the left as if shoved by an invisible force. When he spun full around, he hauled his gun from the holster, turned, and fired. I couldn't see what he fired at because his big frame blocked the shot. He staggered to his right and fired three of four times while on the move. Now tucked beside his vehicle on the passenger side, the woman came into view. She teetered as if drunk and stumbled into the speeding traffic. A black Dodge Challenger barreled into her. Through her is more like it.

I sucked in air and jumped back from my laptop. The woman was in view one second, and then poof. The challenger was barely visible, it took so long to stop. Boulder crawled from the side of the S.U.V. and held his injured shoulder. He'd been shot. He bowed and shook his head slowly. The video ended. I rolled to my back and closed my eyes. What a horrible sight. What a brutal way for someone to die. And to think Boulder carried that death around with him day after day.

I wondered what else he carried with him—what other horrors he'd seen and participated in. I don't know how he stayed in law enforcement.

I reached for Norma Jean and brought her to my chest. I needed to watch the video again and then look for a connection to the gang in town. If there wasn't one, it meant I had to keep searching. But first, I needed a moment. Holding Norma tight, I opened my eyes and stared at the ceiling for five minutes.

When I recovered, I sat back in the cross-legged position and watched the video two more times. Tough shit if I missed something, I couldn't watch it a fourth time. Rather than go back to the text of the story, I checked out the still photos taken after the event. In the first shot, the driver's door to the Tercel was open. Flares had been laid out all over the freeway. Obviously, the police were forced to shut the freeway down. The front end of an ambulance was in the shot. Boulder spoke with two men in suits. Superiors would be my guess.

The next picture was shot from the opposite side. This pic revealed a far more chaotic scene with several first responders. I scanned the faces, unsure as to what I was actually looking for. It was hopeless. I didn't know what the hell I was doing. I heard the voices of both Boulder and Deputy Tawanna telling me to butt out. Maybe I should.

The third picture looked as though the photographer moved into the center of the freeway and snapped the photo. The Tercel door was closed in the picture. A closed body bag lay on a stretcher. My heart rate bumped up. The rear of the ambulance was in full view and what I saw stopped me cold. Two paramedics stood bent over someone that sat on the back edge of the ambulance. That someone was a child. A little boy that couldn't have been more than eight or nine years old.

Oh shit, she had a son!

The little boy sat under a blanket. It was difficult to make out, but more than likely, he was crying. I sat back and thought a moment. This didn't bring the connection of Boulder and Jesse Arlo into focus, but something gnawed at me. I scrolled to the top of the photo and read the date. July 2005. Oh'five, seventeen years ago. I was a newborn. If the little boy was, say, eight years old...

I entered the mother's name; Jane Smithers into a search window and zeroed in on as much as I could about her prior to the accident. Most of the stories related to the accident and gave minimal background on the woman. Apparently, she had a substance abuse problem and had been arrested several times for minor possessions. She had trouble holding down steady work and was on the brink of losing her only son to social services.

I whispered the F word as I read her son's name. Jesse. Eight years old at the time of the accident. Twenty-five years old today. I flashed back to the devilish smile Jesse Arlo flashed at the Horse and Buggy. I thought of his two-handed hair comb-through move. I looked back at the little eight-year-old. Yup, no question: young Jesse was Jesse Arlo, and he was in my town with bad intentions for my sheriff after all these years.

I grabbed my hawk carving and rolled to my side.

CHAPTER TWENTY

I'm the hawk, Arlo..., and you're the pigeon.

Chapter Twenty-One

E motionally busted and lacking imagination and sense, I found myself back at the Horse and Buggy bar. Once again, Tyler, the bouncer, stood sentry at the entrance. Lucy, the bartender, came out. They bumped fists then Lucy dug a pack of smokes out of her front jeans pocket. Tyler declined the cigarette Lucy offered. She lit up, bent her leg at the knee, and put her heel to the wall. She sent a plume of smoke up to the skies. She kept her head up, probably checking out the stars.

The Chrysler 300 was at the far end of the lot. The crew was inside the bar, at least one member anyway. Why would they wait so long to make their move, I wondered? Were they waiting on a payment? Equipment? Or maybe they had to get the go-ahead from a boss higher up. Maybe someone in L.A. was calling the shots? Truth was I had no clue. Give me languages and sciences, and I'm practically an expert. But police work, not a chance.

I wasn't sure if I should approach Tyler and Lucy and ask if any of the 300 crew was inside or wait until Lucy went back inside and then go to the bar like the time before. I really had no clue what to do, so I sat and watched. They shared a few laughs as Lucy burned through her smoke. After she butted it out, she gave Tyler a hug and went back inside.

I was going in. I had my hand on the door handle when Kyle walked up to Tyler. He came from the south side.

What the—

Tyler IDd Kyle. Kyle's fake I.D. somehow passed muster because Tyler handed it back to him and let him go inside. Now, what was I to do? What the hell was Kyle doing there? My blood was spiking. I saw flashes of our bullshit afternoon encounter. It was on a reel that looped. The snap of the condom. The 'whatever' leaving his lips. Screw him. If he had anything to do with this...

Maybe he was just grabbing a beer by himself but out here in Moreford? I didn't think so. I wondered if he was connected to my Boulder case. I shocked myself that I referred to it as a case at all. I was here for the sheriff, but now I was curious about Kyle. Maybe his buddies had fake I.D., and they were already inside. It had to be something like that.

I stepped out of the truck but ducked back in when an S.U.V. crept into the lot from the north. The cherries on top of the vehicle were the reason I hopped back into my truck. I slunk down and peered over the steering wheel. There he was, the man himself, Sheriff Boulder on the bar, which was lucky for me. He'd have recognized my truck for sure if he'd glanced my way. He and Tyler exchanged nods of the heads as Boulder moved past.

The sheriff found a spot at the end of the lot and shut his vehicle down. As he walked toward the bar, a man approached him. It was the big thick-necked member of the 300 crew. Tyler had just left his post and went inside the bar. I stayed put and watched as Boulder and the big man had words. It didn't appear hostile, but both men seemed ready for action. A shift of the boot for balance, a deliberate amount of spacing. To me, they looked like two men on the brink of a fight but both pretending they were not. I didn't like it. A shadow slid across the blacktop from behind Boulder, then disappeared. Boulder didn't notice it. I began to wonder if I imagined it when from between two parked sedans charged a dark figure.

"Hey!" I shouted, but my windows were up. I leaped out of my truck and called but was too late. The dark figure was on Boulder. The way the sheriff's legs buckled suggested he'd either been smacked with precision with a blunt object, been injected with something, or zapped by a taser. I jumped to the pavement and sprinted toward the group.

"Hey! Leave him alone!"

I sprinted past the entrance. The two men were walk-dragging the sheriff toward a plain white panel van. The side door slid open. I was gaining on the group. Norma Jean was in my right hand. I got within just under twenty feet and let Norma fly. She flew end over end until her blade sunk into the hamstring of the big man. He cried out and looked back at his leg. He was forced to drop his end of Boulder while he pulled the blade from his leg. Dark liquid spread down his tight jeans.

"You stupid bitch!" He said, looking from his leg to me. I had The Girl in my hand with my right arm cocked, still on the run but within single-digit feet of the guy. The Girl was going into his throat. I screamed something unintelligible mid-hurl but then was slammed by something from my right side. I flew through the air and landed hard on my left side. The wind rushed out of my lungs. The Girl flew from my grasp. A heavy weight was on top of me. When my focus cleared I saw Kyle looking down at me.

"Kyle! You tackled me? What the fuck are you doing?"

"I'm sorry, Chloe. You shouldn't be here. You should have stayed out of this."

With a knee across my upper torso, he had me pinned.

"Get the fuck off me. They're taking the sheriff, you idiot!"

"Sorry, Chloe, but you should have minded your own business. Seriously!"

He drew his hand back in a fist, ready to punch down at me.

You're gonna knock me out, asshole?

I'd never taken a jiujitsu class, nor stepped foot in a gym. But I'd watched untold hours of Youtube videos on the art. The art is for the smaller man to neutralize the larger. Or, in my case, the smaller wolverine of a high school senior girl to overpower the two-faced premature ejaculator. He thought he had me controlled by the knee that pinned me. But I'd thrust my hips skyward, rotate to my left and shove my butt backward with the aid of my feet. This would all happen in under a second. His overconfidence in being 'the bigger man' would help as well. Sure, Kyle's bigger than me, but no way was he as fast—nor driven.

Ready! Engage Chloe!

But there was no need. Suddenly he was no longer in my sight line, and his body weight was gone. Where his head had been was something like a size seven Doc Martin boot. Lucy kicked him so hard in the side of the head that he flew off me and landed a few feet away. I rolled over and got to my feet and trailed Lucy as she pursued Kyle. He crawled on hands and knees alongside a 70s model Cadillac. Lucy caught up to him.

"We punching girls in the face now, asshole?" She grabbed a handful of his hair, pinned his head to the caddy, and drove her knee into his temple. Two sounds broke the scene: *thwack-boom*. The knee connected with the head, then the head smashed into the Cadillac near the back tire.

"Right on, sister!" I said. Lucy turned away from the unconscious heap. We were inches apart. I felt her hot breath on my face. Most of her hair fell in front of her face. Her eyes looked like a wild animal's and suggested she was ready to take on more opponents should they test her.

"Thanks, Lucy," I said, admiring the shit out of her. She gave me a quick nod.

"The panel van's tires squealed on the pavement as they pulled out of the spot and took off down the lot. The Chrysler 300 pulled up fast and hugged the van's back bumper.

"Shit! Boulder!" I screamed. "No!"

"What the hell, Chloe? They take the sheriff?"

"Yes, Lucy. God damn it." Spotting The Girl, I scooped her up and sprinted down after the Chrysler. I let The Girl loose. She sailed end over end, knocked out the right rear brake light then ricocheted off to the right. I bent over, with hands on knees, and stared, helpless. Lucy caught up to me. She grabbed me by the shoulders and stood me upright.

"I'm good," I said and pulled out my phone. My hand shook as I tapped in the numbers of Deputy Raven Tawanna.

"What do you want, Chloe?"

"They've got...got Boulder. They took him. Those fucking guys."

"Shit. Where are you?"

I told her.

"We'll talk about that later. Are they in the 300?"

"Boulder's in a white panel van. License plate was, shit hang on. I squeezed my eyes shut...S, B—"

"What? S, D? Repeat, please," the deputy said.

"Shit, ah, Sierra, Bravo, Lima, Six, Four...shit Six, Four—"

"Three, five," Lucy added.

"That's right, Sierra, Bravo, Lima, Six, Four, Three, Five. California plate." I could hear Raven calling dispatch or someone like that.

"Got it. It's a rental from Moreford Daily Rentals. Stay put, Chloe. I'm almost there. Do not leave and do not pursue."

I hung up. When I turned back to Lucy, Tyler was standing with her. Lucy must have filled him in.

"Fuck me, I feel like shit. I just went for a piss, and all that went down? Son of a bitch."

"Son of a bitch is right," I said. "We coulda used your help."

"Boulder's a good dude. I like him," he said. "How do you think they got him?"

"Chloroform? Taser? Who knows? It just happened too fast to be a blow to the head. I mean, you'd have to—"

"Hit him with a lead pipe, and more than once," Tyler added. "But I tell ya what, when Boulder wakes up, they're gonna wish they'd taken someone else."

"Hell yeah, they are," Lucy said. "They took the wrong guy."

Kyle started moaning on the ground. Our heads turned in unison. We'd forgotten about him. He'd pushed himself to one knee by the time I got to him. I balled up my fist and punched him square in the nose. My hand vibrated. I hope I didn't break anything. He sat back on his ass and clutched his face in both hands. I went in for more, but Lucy and Tyler pulled me away. "We need him awake, sweetheart," Tyler said calmly in my ear. "Easy now."

Satisfied with my assurances, Tyler let me go. Lucy stood between Kyle and me. I walked over to Norma Jean and cleaned her off on the cuff of my jeans. Tyler and Lucy visibly relaxed as I slid her into the scabbard. I fast walked down the lot and found The Girl sitting on the pavement. She rested atop a few shards of red tail light plastic. Returning The Girl to her home, I rejoined the group

"Fuck, Chloe, I think you broke my nose," said Kyle.

"Good," I said, clenching and unclenching my fist.

Deputy Tawanna's vehicle came in hot. She skided to a stop a foot from where we stood. Her boots clopped with purpose towards us.

"Somebody talk. Just one of you."

The deputy said nothing as I spread the story before her. Her only movement was to put Kyle in handcuffs and shove him into the back of her vehicle. She got Lucy and Tyler to agree to swing by the station the following day to give full statements. Once they went back to work, she put her focus on me.

"Deputy Burris is up north visiting his dad. Lung cancer. Speaking of parents, sorry to hear about Joselyn. She gonna be all right?'

"Uh-huh."

"Good," she paused. "You're in this now. We're gonna reach out to all other departments, but I don't think we have a lot of time."

I nodded.

She used her chin to point to her vehicle. "I'll get what we need out of your boyfriend there and then—"

"Don't fucking call him that. I can't believe I let that fucker touch me."

"Whatever, I may need your help."

"Name it," I said.

"I know knives are your thing but can you still shoot? I know you were too young for your daddy to teach you, but I know you get out to the range every three months or so."

"How the hell do you know that?"

Her face read nothing other than that my question was a dumb one.

Cops. Small towns.

"I can shoot fine, especially when I have a reason," I told her.

"You got a piece, or do you rent when you're at the range?"

"Rent."

"The old man didn't leave any ordinance behind?"

"Momma didn't want his weapons around—sold everything," I said. "Then donated the money to Jack Daniels and half the bars around town."

"Go home. Hopefully, I won't need you, but if I do, it'll probably cost me my job." She paused. "But this is Sheriff Boulder we're taking here."

I moved on autopilot. My back was to Raven when she received a call. Her tone brought me back to her.

"You're in way over your head, asshole. Return the sheriff before it's too late."

I got close enough to hear the other party's voice. It was Jesse, the Josh Brolin look-a-like. I was surprised Tawanna allowed me to listen in.

"*Shut up and listen,*" he said. "*No outside law enforcement. No Feds, no cops from other counties, nothin' or the beloved sheriff dies early.*"

"What do you mean dies early?" Tawanna asked. Her voice was empty of emotion.

"*It means we're gonna have a little fun with the big man...and then—*"

I wanted to rip the phone from her hand and shout every swear word I'd ever learned.

"Trade," she said. My eyes went wide as I looked at her. "You and your boys can have your way with me instead. Let the sheriff go. People in this town like the sheriff...a lot."

"*How absolutely noble. They can't be paying you enough for a move like that. Ooh, forget nobility, it must be...are you in love with your boss? How truly Hallmark.*"

"Trade asshole, let's go."

There was a reason I called her Deputy Bad Ass.

"*Thanks for the offer but no deal.*"

The deputy's eyebrows worked into a frown. It was the first sign of emotion during the call. There was a lengthy pause. I was afraid he'd hang up. It was as if Raven played it right to the line. When she spoke, her voice was a little softer. Not intimate, but the way a mother might scold a child in a way she'd garner his full attention.

"Boulder killed her in self-defense you know—your mother. It wasn't his fault."

My mouth fell open. The deputy already knew what I knew, "what the fuck!" When Raven put a 'shh' finger to her lips. I gathered control but felt a massive howl building inside my rib cage.

"You were what, eight years old when it happened? And you were in the

128

back seat. You were young enough to still be hopeful. Maybe you knew you were poor, maybe not. But you probably had no idea your mother was a meth-head."

She paused a moment. Now I totally freaked that he'd hang up the phone, and we'd be no closer to finding...

"Is it me, or are you breathing just a little bit harder, Arlo?" she said. "Boulder was simply going to run her I.D. he was heading back to his patrol unit—didn't suspect shit. But your mother, high as fuck, stepped out of the Tercel and opened fire. Boulder caught one in the shoulder before returning fire."

Another pause. Shorter this time.

"Like I said, self defense. Boulder was cleared. Clean shoot."

"You don't know shit!" His voice was a guttural growl.

"But there was little Jesse playing with his favorite toy truck in the back seat. It had to be horrible hearing your mother getting smoked like that. Dead before her body met concrete."

"You'll pay, you fucking bitch!"

"So trade. Take it out on me. You ever had a native girl before? I doubt it. Take me for a ride. I'll show you wild."

We were way past rattling a guy's cage. Arlo was totally coming undone. Still through it all, Deputy Tawanna kept her voice level, like a lawyer telling her client to take the plea deal.

"You keep this up, you're looking at kidnapping, torture, mayhem, and murder," she said. "Maybe."

I shuddered.

"But you let him go and take this brown girl, we're only talking sexual assault."

"You don't make the rules," he shouted. *"I'm in con—"*

"Control? Aw, that's cute. I bet your little nostrils are flaring right now."

"You crazy bitch!" He said.

"Yes. Yes. Yes, I'm crazy, so come on, stud, take this crazy bitch because the window of opportunity is closing."

Her phone beeped three times.

"Shit. Shit, he hung up," I said. "The sheriff is screwed. Why did you provoke him like that?"

"Quiet!"

Now you show emotion.

My words stayed in my mouth.

"I've taken the focus off the sheriff. Jesse needed to be reminded it was self-defense when his mother was killed. And who knows, maybe he sends out his little kidnapping crew to grab me. If so, I get close and kill them all," she said. "Nobody's getting arrested. And we never had this conversation."

I exhaled deeply. "But what if he just snaps and kills the sheriff?" I had tears in my eyes. "This is revenge, plain and simple. I saw the video. This asshole has waited seventeen years for this. Boulder doesn't stand a—"

"He won't. I've done this before."

I turned from her and ran my hands through my hair, and paced.

"I just figured this shit out. Why didn't you guys let me know you knew what this was about?"

The deputy looked at me like I was an alien. "You mean how, through the miracle of police work, did we find out exactly who this asshole is, and why didn't we clue in the great Chloe Savannah immediately upon our findings?"

I looked down at my boots. "Sorry, you're right, you're right. I'm just freaking out, is all."

"Understood. I'm going to squeeze that little fuck in my vehicle until he tells me where Boulder is. Then we move. I may still need you, but you've got to woman-up girl. Stop the tears and stop the fucking millennial hysterics, I hate that shit."

"Done," I said, thumbing Norma Jean. "I'm Gen Z, but done. Call me. I'll be ready."

My truck roared to life. I drove home and stressed about Boulder the whole way. I lost my father at a young age. Now it felt like I was about to lose an uncle...or second father. Before climbing into bed, I checked on the one question I needed to answer. Why was Jesse's last name Arlo and his mother's Smithers? Deep mining of the story revealed that Jesse kept his father's surname. The day his mother shot at the C.H.P. officer who pulled her over, she was stoned on meth and attempting to move her son out of state away from her ex-husband, who had sole custody of young Jesse.

I was wide awake with my thoughts all tumbling and scrambling over one another. Sleep wasn't coming. I waited until about four in the morning for Raven Tawanna's call. Nothing. I texted her three question marks.

"Nothing tonight. Go to sleep." Came the response.

Chapter Twenty-Two

Sleep came easier than I thought it would, seeing as I had both the sheriff and Momma on my mind when my head hit the pillow. I slept hard and didn't move an inch until the sun bore into my bedroom at seven a.m. I was surprisingly refreshed for only three hours of sleep. I checked my phone in case I missed a text from Raven. Still nothing, so I called.

"Anything?" There was a ton of noise in the background.

"Just a reminder text message warning me to keep Feds and other law enforcement away from this."

"So he reached out. That's good, right?"

"Yes," she said.

"Now what?"

"We wait."

I ain't waiting.

"Okay, keep me in the loop."

"It's under control. Go see your mother."

I hung up without saying goodbye because the 'go see your mother' comment pissed me off and I didn't trust my mouth. I was planning on going by the hospital right after breakfast but got another idea. Unfortunately, I wasn't the only one with the idea.

When I parked my truck at Moreford Daily Rentals, Deputy Tawanna pulled in and parked beside me. Her cool stare chilled me. No words, just the look. We walked together toward the main office. I got to the door first and held it open for her. I wasn't thanked for the overture.

"How may I help you, ladies?" A short man with a comb-over and bulge at the middle shared a huge salesman grin with us. His eyes briefly flicked with concern at seeing Raven's uniform, but he did his best to mask it. He was definitely guilty of something.

The deputy pulled a printout from her inside jacket pocket and laid it on the counter.

"Tell me about the guys or guy that rented this van."

He frowned a moment then his comb-over slid backward on his round skull. After letting out a deep sigh he sang like a canary. Two guys came in. One big, one quiet. They didn't talk much but what little they said gave him the creeps.

"You always rent to clientele like that?" Tawanna asked.

"No law against it. I'm just saying I didn't like them, is all. And," he paused and ran a hand over his weak goatee. "My hunch about them must have been right seeing as there's a sheriff's deputy standing in front of me."

"I don't suppose they mentioned what they were planning to do with the van or where they were going?"

"No, they certainly did not. I tried to make conversation on it but they stayed pretty locked up on the matter."

Raven considered her next question. The man turned to me. "And what about you, pretty lady, are you a deputy as well?"

"She's my niece. Doing a ride-along. Listen, how long did they say they were renting for?"

"They said a week, but maybe less."

I didn't like that. It meant they were planning on holding Boulder for at least that long and that could only mean torture. Raven held her hat in front of her and tapped her finger on the brim.

"Mind if I look at the paperwork on the rental?"

"Sure, by all means." He shuffled the paperwork across to Raven as quick as he could so he could get back to me.

"So how's the ride-along going? Will we see you in uniform one day?"

"Military uniform, maybe. I'm going to join the marines, go to sniper school and rack up some kills for America."

"Christ on a biscuit, no! You're far too pretty for that young lady."

"Honor," I said.

The man wore a look somewhere between terrified and disappointed. Deputy Tawanna asked for a copy of the paperwork. Mr. Salesman was all too happy to head back to his copier in his office. When we were alone, Raven asked if I was having fun?

"Not in the least," I said.

"Good."

"I guess Kyle didn't cough anything up?"

"He's a small player. They paid him to keep an eye on Boulder and report his movements. I'm convinced that's the extent of his involvement in this thing. He doesn't know where they took the sheriff. Trust me, if he knew, we'd know."

"Well," I said. "I hope you hurt him."

"He already had a concussion and busted nose," she said. "Know anything about it?"

"Fuck yeah, I do."

"Good girl," she said.

Mr. Salesman's name was actually Ned Seavers. He handed the copies to Raven with enthusiasm.

"Ya know I'm glad my hunch paid off. I'm so glad I called you guys," he said.

"What do you mean?" Raven asked.

"Well, I called the sheriff and told him I had an uneasy feeling about those fellas. I thought that's why you're here now. Sheriff Boulder didn't tell you?"

"That's what he was doing out at the bar," I blurted. "Checking out—"

"Thank you so much for your time, Mr. Seavers. Anything else, holler," Raven said.

* * *

"You don't need to tell the interviewee everything you know, Chloe. It's why I shut you up back there."

CHAPTER TWENTY-TWO

"I figured. Sorry about that."

We leaned against her unit. Her back was to the vehicle with hands in pockets. I leaned sideways on the truck with my arms folded.

"That stuff about offering yourself to the crew. Would you—"

I let the question hang, but Raven didn't answer right away.

"It was all talk to get their location, Chloe. Don't read anything else into it. Coming up poor on the reserve didn't ruin me. Neither has working the job. I'm not damaged goods—not seriously anyway," she paused and blew out a breath. "I'm just officer Bad Ass."

"Hey, I thought I wasn't allowed to call you that."

"You're not. And I'll shoot you before you get either one of those knives out if you do."

The warm breeze blew our hair around our faces. Hers more than mine since mine's so thick. I wanted to tell her how scared I was for the sheriff but remembered her 'buck up' speech from the previous day.

"So, Kyle," she said.

"Fuck Kyle."

"Did you?"

"What? No, not that it's any of your business. Shouldn't we focus on Boulder?"

"You need to learn to listen when wisdom is coming your way, kid."

I buttoned my lip.

"How far you went with the guy is irrelevant. The point is you were interested in him. I'm here to tell you you'll pick the wrong guy again down the road. I mean no insult, it happens to the healthiest of us. Just make sure you learn from your fuck ups."

I felt my face getting hot.

"Sometimes the sweetest guys are assholes. It can take a minute to look behind the mask. But in your case, you've got Joselyn bringing all kinds of assholes around."

"You know better than anyone else," I said, thinking back to the giant she killed in my hallway.

"What I'm trying to say is they're not all dicks. Kyle is a complete idiot, but he's not evil—just dumb and weak of character. Don't kill yourself over it and don't lump all men in the A-hole category. Just keep sifting through the rough, and you'll find your diamond."

A silence fell between us. I felt ten feet tall and near invincible having Raven Tawanna as an ally.

"We did fool around. Didn't go all the way through," I said. "I would have, but he—" I stopped myself.

"What? Got rough with you?"

"Oh my god no he just went…long before me, if you know what I mean."

"Mr. One minute, man, huh?" she asked.

"Minute? Shit. He didn't even get to the gate," I said. "But at least he said it was cause I'm so hot."

"Oh, that line. Priceless."

We didn't speak for a long two-minute stretch. We looked over at Ned Seavers, who was giddy with himself for renting an R.V. to a couple in their late seventies.

"Forget Kyle," she said finally.

"Forgotten," I said.

"And if you do leave after all this shit is done. I'm with Shayna. I'll look in on Joselyn—maybe try to get her into a program."

"My god, Shayna told you—what is it with this tiny assed town?"

"It was two people talking who care about you. If that pisses you off, you're a damn fool. You're loved, dumb ass. It ain't always you against the world."

More silence fell between us. These bitches were making it so hard to leave.

"You know I looked up your name, your last name, on a Chickasaw website."

I looked at Raven but she kept her eyes forward and didn't register my comment in any way.

"Tawanna, Beautiful Running Water," I said.

"Uh-huh."

More silence.

"It's a beautiful name," I said. "But then I looked a little deeper."

The deputy slowly turned and put warning eyes on me. Scary, but I kept going.

"Your name also translates as 'Little Princess.'"

"You'll catch a bullet if you ever call me that," she said.

"Okay, okay, you're so hostile," I smiled.

The silence was brief this time.

"We need to focus on Boulder," She asked, pushing off the vehicle.

"Totally agree," I said. She gave me a final warning look. I scrapped my smile.

"Good, now get your ass to school. I don't want to see you moping around here because you're two credits short and have to attend summer school."

Chapter Twenty-Three

I knew I should go visit Momma but Raven's rib about graduating put school back on my radar. I figured I'd check in. A quick hello to some of the teachers, play the part of the invested student and check there weren't any missed assignments that needed doing—seemed like a sound plan. I'd go see Momma after that.

I did the full class of A.P. chemistry, then made a twenty-minute appearance at Spanish. After that, I headed in the direction of Ms. Mackenzie my guidance counselor's office. I was two doors down from hers when principal Cross poked his head out his office door.

"Chloe, ya got a minute?"

"Sure, Mr. Cross."

He opened the door wider and allowed me entry with an upturned palm. I sat down in the same seat as I had the last time I was in.

"What's up? I was just on my way to see Ms. Mackenzie."

"Okay, this won't take long. First, I want to say how sorry I am at hearing about Joselyn. Any update? Is she going to be all right?"

"As far as I know, she'll be fine. I'm heading there after school," I said, crossing a leg over my knee.

"Good, well, on behalf of me and the staff here, we're praying for her."

"Thank you. I'll pass that on to her."

He took his eyes off me and fidgeted with an unopened box of paper clips. "Chloe, I also heard about the other night out at the Horse and Buggy."

Here we go.

"Now, I'm not judging or gonna come down on you for fraternizing at a

138

bar while underage, that's not my department. But Kyle Douglas was out there too, am I correct?"

"You know he was, so you're either seeing if I'll lie about his being there, or you're playing dumb. What's going on here Cross?"

"Mr. Cross."

"Cross," I said. My blood began to simmer.

"You're right. I shouldn't play games. You're too smart for that."

He sat back and took the paper clips with him. "I've been on the phone with his parents and they, *we're* concerned you might press charges, but you seem to be okay, to me. So—"

"Press charges?"

"I believe he bumped into—you were knocked to the ground or something?"

I uncrossed my legs, put both boot soles on the floor, and sat forward with my forearms on my thighs. "You're all worried I'll press charges because six foot and one inch Kyle Douglas tackled me to the ground?"

"Well, it's just that—look Kyle has a very bright athletic future. Half a dozen colleges want him on their water polo team and—"

I held up my palm and stopped him cold. "So you're saying Mr. Aw shucks, good looking Kyle with the Hollywood chin, thick shiny locks, and dimples any grandmother would endlessly pinch has a bright future. And this future could be ruined by the little mix-raced girl pressing charges? Ha, what a joke."

"I never mentioned race Chloe, never mentioned race. But to be fair, the Douglas family has a very good, long upstanding reputation in this community and they've—"

"And the Savannahs have a mother who's a drunk."

"That's, that's not what I'm saying." His face flushed. He dropped the paper clip box on his desk. It tumbled off and cracked open on the floor. We both ignored the hundred pieces of metal as they fanned out.

"And my father. Are you ready for this?"

"Chloe, don't."

"My father was a stop-loss soldier, which meant he had to work beyond his contract."

"I know what stop-loss is, Chloe," he said it like he was plugging leaks in a boat and didn't have enough fingers.

"Did you know that there was an appropriations bill? It granted soldiers that were forced to grind it out over in Iraq and Afghanistan—my father fought in both thank you very much—it granted them a salary bump of up to five hundred bucks a month. Ooh ah, sign me up."

"Chloe, this is not necessary."

"But at first the bill only covered soldiers that fought in two-thousand nine and then up to twenty-eleven."

"This is not relevant to—"

"Hang on, Cross," I said. "But it wasn't until later that they decided men like my father that had been in the fight since nine-eleven should receive back-pay. My daddy had severe PTSD, but he was to be paid a whopping two-fifty, not the full five hundred. Shit pay, but he really needed the money. Momma," I said, "Sober Momma needed the money. She was raising a lovely daughter, after all. So, the government, being the government, screwed up the paperwork and the checks didn't start coming until June fifteenth of twenty-ten," I said. "Three weeks after my daddy killed himself. One bullet. Under the chin and out the top of the skull."

"Dang it, Chloe!" He said and pounded the desk with the flat of his palm.

"I'm not saying the money would have saved his life, he was already pretty much a dead man walking due to what he saw over there…giving all for his country. But maybe it would have brought a little sunshine to one of his remaining dim, dark days."

Cross's little concave chest heaved up and down.

"So I think you're saying suicidal father and drunk mother rank far below the, as you said, upstanding Douglas clan," I paused. I leaned in so he could feel the heat coming off me.

"I don't give a shit about Kyle and his upstanding Lilly white family. I'm sure they've promised you a new gymnasium if you make sure I stay quiet. Or maybe you're banging Mrs. Douglas and she needs a favor. Who knows?"

"How dare you!" He stood and jammed an index finger at me.

"You protest too much, Mike," I said. "But I don't care." I stood up on

140

my side of the desk. No way was he going to look down at me, literally or metaphorically. Veins bulged from his rouge neck as he fussed and stammered grasping for words. I didn't give him the chance.

"Here's how stupid you are, Cross. Assault charges from me pale massively in comparison to Kyle's real troubles. And second, a veteran, a stop loss veteran is far more upstanding than Mr. fucking Douglas or any businessman for that matter."

We stared at each other. I'd say the level of hatred in our eyes was even. He narrowed his eyes and opened his mouth, but I cut him off.

"And all so a white boy can splash around in a pool with other boys and toss a ball in a net. You're pathetic."

He gritted his teeth and spoke as if he was trying to keep his voice down and his temper cool. "You are way out of line missy! You millennials think you're so much better than everybody else. Just wait until you hit the real world, young lady."

"I don't give a shit about millennials, Cross. I'm Generation Z." I let out a laugh meant to humiliate him. "Boy, you really have your finger on the pulse of your students."

"Ah, who gives a crap." He waved a hand in front of his face. "Listen, you want to take on the Douglas family good luck with that."

"Take on?" I chuckled. "Cross, you're an uninformed little man with childlike erroneous assumptions," I said. "I should have known your Wally Clever routine was all an act. All show…and no…fucking…go."

I slammed the door behind me on the way out, hoping the frosted glass would shatter for emphasis—like in the movies. It did not. I did however decide a visit to councilor Mackenzie wasn't a great idea in that moment.

Chapter Twenty-Four

The blow up with Cross landed me back at the hospital three hours earlier than planned. I found myself really wanting to see Momma. We went through hell together nearly dying at the hands of a giant. Then I had to go and possibly push her into a stroke. Guilt, love, regret, shame, anger, you name it, I felt the entire spectrum of emotions.

Momma's bed was up at an angle, and two pillows helped prop her up. Aside from bruising, her eyes looked clearer than they had in a long time. We looked at each other. Both of us wore looks full of hope and possibility.

"Well, you're sure looking better, Momma," I said. "How do you feel?"

I kissed her lightly on the cheek, then sat on the edge of the bed. I took her hand and gently enveloped it in both of mine. Her hand was small and warm. I was immediately thrust back to a time when I was young, and she walked me to school. When her hand was the larger and mine the smaller…back when Daddy was still with us.

"Feelin' a little tired, a little sore but much better than when you saw me last."

Her smile was weak and for the first time, I noticed her laugh lines had deepened.

"They say when you can come home?" I asked.

"Should have been today but there's something going on with my blood."

Footfalls approached, "Blood pressure's just a little too high for my liking but we're on top of it," Doctor Griffiths said, breezing into the room. She wore her white doctor's coat over a steel blue button-up blouse. Her slacks were a similar blue color.

"We'll keep her here another night just to be safe, then she should be good to go tomorrow, probably late morning."

"How's my blood pressure high when I'm just laying here doin' nothing?" Momma asked.

"That's why you'll be a guest here another night." The doctor leaned close as she said it. With a penlight she checked Momma's eyes. Next, she pushed up Momma's hospital gown sleeve and strapped the sphygmomanometer to Momma's arm, and checked her blood pressure.

"Hmm, better, but not loving it," she said, unlatching the velcro armband. Momma open and closed her hand a few times. I was glad she had the mobility. After running us through the upcoming schedule, Doctor Griffiths left us.

"I know that look, Momma. Whatever conversation you want to have, please keep it light. We have your blood pressure to think about."

"I'm fine," she said. "But okay. It's about you leaving."

"Nope, not having that conversation, no way." I stood to leave.

"I want you to go," she said. She'd leaned forward from her pillows when she said and it caused her pain. She tried to hide it but I knew her too well.

"Easy, Momma. Here, sit back. Relax," I said and adjusted her pillows.

"I'm your mother, and I've had a stroke. Now show me respect and shut up and listen."

We held each other's look. My temperature was rising, and she knew it but held her ground. Five seconds later, a slight grin formed at the corner of her mouth. We both laughed at the same time. But it was more of a whisper type snicker.

"Okay, Joselyn, you have the floor. But the minute you get intense, I'm leaving...for your own good."

"Good," she said and scratched at the mattress beside her. The gesture reminded me of a kitten pawing at kitty litter. I suppose it was all the mobility she could muster in the moment. I sat back down on the edge ready to listen or bolt, depending.

"You know I love you and you know your father loved you very much, in spite of what he did."

My face grew incredibly hot.

"The last place your father should have been was on a battlefield taking lives," she said. "And witnessing all that came with those conflicts. He was such a gentle man. War was against his nature."

"I know this, Momma. Can we just—"

"He was so torn apart that I believe a meanness was growing inside of him. A meanness forged by—well, you know. But that evil, vile fucking, thing began to fester, and although he never raised a hand to me or you, I truly believe…" her words caught. Tears rolled down both our cheeks. I reached for the tissues at the side of her bed and handed them to her. For my tears, I used my jacket sleeve.

"Aah," she sighed. "God dammit. As I was saying, your father, I truly believe he feared that he would one day physically harm us. That's how powerful the demon inside him had become. So he decided there was only one way to keep us safe, and that was to exit this earth. I miss him every day and I'm so sorry you were robbed of a decent, loving father and were saddled with…" She lost it again.

"Saddled with an alcoholic mother. I'm ashamed of myself and I know, as loving as he is," she gulped. "He's disappointed in me too."

"Okay, Momma, I'm a mess. Can we just stop this conversation? Please?" I put my face in my hands and let Niagara Falls flow out of me. It seemed like hours before I pulled out of it.

"I'm almost finished," she said. "What I wanted to say was you were right. I've been selfish. When you said you were leaving I panicked and thought only of myself. Reason number five-hundred why I'm a shitty mom. But," she paused. "I want you to go. Honestly. Truly, I want you to go for two reasons. One is that it is not your job to look after me. And two; ever since you were little, half your soul has lived here in Bucksville and the other half," she smiled. "Has been out there somewhere. I see you roaming around this planet stopping here, traveling there, until god knows where you'll end up."

I exhaled deeply. The yin and yang of emotions flooding through me were freedom and guilt in equal measure. If I had any more tears, I'd have shed them in that moment. But I was done. I stood, leaned into Momma, and gave her a huge hug.

"Thank you," I whispered.

"Don't do that. Thank you, daughter. Thank you."

Chapter Twenty-Five

I'm not a completely heartless person. Obviously, I'd stick around and help Momma through her rehab stage but once she's significantly convalesced I'm on a plane. I allowed myself a dumb grin as I walked to my truck. I checked the time. My shift at the laundromat was coming up. I was imagining my final shift at the laundromat and picturing my co-worker Skinny Dave. He'd be pissed at having to cover extra shifts until they find my replacement but, hey, it's extra cash in his pocket. As a favor to the boss Joe English, I'll have to play Ms. Bright Side and explain that to Skinny Dave.

Shit! I'd totally forgotten about Sheriff Boulder. Guilt returned. I pulled my phone out and called Raven Tawanna, the Little Princess. I didn't give two shits that I was driving while making the call. Boulder was priority one.

"Hey, kid. Nothing yet," Raven said. "I swung by the motel they stayed at but they've checked out."

"Dang it! This is bad. Isn't the first forty-eight like a big deal or something? Like that TV show."

"I'm not talking to you about TV shows, Chloe. Keep checking with me and I'll let you know when I've got something."

"So…not…satisfying!"

She didn't say anything. Tawanna never did if it didn't move a conversation forward.

"Okay, well I'm going to work but I can leave any time if you find out where he is."

"Copy that."

"What about his house? I'm sure that was the first place you looked, but—or what about the motel? I know you checked, but I know the front desk lady, I can call if—"

"If you took someone, would you go to the obvious places, Chloe?"

I sighed heavily and nearly ran a red light. I locked my breaks up. "Shhhhhhit!"

"I heard that. Hands-free Chloe, don't be stupid."

The phone beeped three times. Officer Bad Ass had killed the call.

Five minutes later I walked into Joe's Laundromat. Skinny Dave barely looked at me as he said 'hey' and headed for the door.

"Hey, Skinny?"

"S'up?"

"Are you looking for extra shifts? A little extra cash for some sweet pegs for your bike or something?"

"Fuck no, why?"

"No reason, just shootin' the shit."

"Yeah, well, I'm trying to get outta here, Chloe." He turned to go but stopped by the door.

"Oh, some creepy dude came by askin' for ya."

"Creepy how?" I asked.

"I dunno. Jacked up haircut like a nerd and orange-colored eyes like fuckin' cat or something."

It's not often my mouth falls open.

"I can see by your face he freaks you out too, huh? If he comes back and he really puts the fear in you, call your sheriff buddy," he said. "Or that smokin' hot Indian deputy."

"Indigenous. And yeah, okay, thanks, Skinny."

The mention of the Quiet One was a knife to the gut. The mention of the sheriff, who'd been taken and was god-knew-where was the twisting of that knife tearing my intestines to shreds. I didn't even realize my hand was on Norma Jean's hilt.

Fuck me.

I functioned on autopilot as I did the take-in laundry. Detergents and softeners seemed to measure themselves out. The machines almost cranked up on their own. I hoisted myself onto my usual washer and sat crossed-legged. Elbows on knees. Face in hands, I thought. I pondered. What the hell was The Quiet One doing away from wherever they were holding Boulder? And why ask for me?

A cold chill slid down my spine as if I stood under an eave and water from an icicle dripped down from above. I was scared. Scared for Momma, Boulder, and me. I hate being scared. It makes me—

"Hey," a voice said, pulling me from my thoughts.

The Quiet One, true to the name I'd given him managed to enter the place and get three feet from me without me hearing him.

"What are you doing here? Your jacket looks clean to me."

I'm sure he didn't buy the false confidence in the edge I gave my voice. I sure didn't. He leaned against an industrial dryer and folded his arms across his chest.

"I came to talk to you."

"Well, since you're here, I'm going first. Where's the sheriff, asshole?"

"In due time," he said.

"Due time is now. Where is he!" My voice was just under a scream.

He smiled. Not a care in the world.

"What do you see in Kyle anyway?"

"What? Nothing. And how the fuck do you know my name and his?" I said.

He stared with a half-grin, like he knew something I didn't and relished it.

"So, you did your homework. You asked around. You went to the library. I don't know or care. Just tell me where Sheriff Boulder is before I call the deputies in."

"Deputy. Singular. Deputy Burris is out of town. That leaves Tawanna."

I stepped down from the washer and faced him, hands at my sides. "You're so impressed with yourself," I said. "So what's next?"

He pushed off the dryer and stood facing me with arms at *his* sides.

"Kyle is a prick, always has been."

"Okay, who are you? You obviously know him, and you're here now to talk to me. Who are you other than some self impressed, quiet...whatever?"

"You really don't remember, do you?"

"Enlighten me."

He took a step closer.

"My hair used to be the color of my eyes," he said. The grin slid from his face.

I flashed back to my sophomore year in high school—nothing. I went back further middle school—still nothing. I went way back, and then an image from an elementary school photo popped up. Red hair...red hair...redhead... Teddy—

"Teddy? Teddy Redhead?"

"It's Watkins, but everyone called me Teddy Redhead, yeah."

"Jesus" was the most intelligent thing I came up with. Teddy was picked on as a kid. There were other redheads, what they call gingers now but for some reason...Or actually, no reason, kids can just be assholes. Images and memories flooded in. Then, they stopped. They stopped on Kyle.

"Oh my god, Teddy, Kyle was your worst tormentor," I said.

"Yeah, Pretty Boy took bullying to the nth degree, Chloe." His thin lips lay in a flat line and his eyes held a quiet rage. I was familiar with the feeling.

"Your face is loaded with recollection. You remember," he said.

I nodded.

"He's going to pay, whether you're with him or not. Just thought you should know."

"I'm not with him. Anyway, you can't just—"

"You were always nice to me, Chloe. I'm a little hurt you didn't recognize me, but—"

"But your hair's jet black now, and we're talking like a decade ago."

"Exactly."

We both stood there. It was like we were back on the playground nine and a half years earlier. I saw the little red haired, red faced boy sitting on the ground, hugging his knees tightly with tears and snot running down his face. I'd often sit with him afterwards. He'd ask me 'why' over and over. I never had an answer for him. Just pity. Sometimes they'd tease me for being his boyfriend. It never got to me though, so they eventually left me alone. But poor Teddy Redhead—Watkins was the weakling in the herd. They never left him alone.

I could tell he was as lost for words as I was. The first washer of my take-ins buzzed. It was the only sound between us. God, it was loud. I felt sorry for Teddy. Pity, anger, sickness, weariness, all of it bundled in an untidy package.

But no way was I going to sit around all day and pity this guy who's living in the past. I snapped back to the present like I'd broken a warlock's spell.

"Where the hell is Sheriff Boulder?" I shouted. "Where are you holding him, Teddy?"

His eyes locked on my body at waist level. I followed his gaze and realized he was locked on Norma Jean. I hadn't even noticed I'd jerked her out and was holding her beside my thigh. My knife hand trembled. In fact, my entire body behaved as though a mini-quake ran through it. He brought his eyes up. I met his gaze and raised Norma threatening.

"Out with it, Teddy. Where the fuck is he? And you better not—"

"Knife or gun, you shouldn't pull either on someone unless you plan on using it," he said far more casually than I would have liked.

"Then you know how serious I am. It doesn't matter that you once lived here and were bullied. Nobody takes our sheriff, not without a fight."

I bent my legs, ready for his attack. He stayed put. More still than a sculpture.

"I'm not here for you, so you can relax."

"Answer me!" I shouted. I lunched forward with a feint to his stomach. He didn't bite at all. Then I flipped my trajectory and came with a downward cross slice meant for his right cheek. It wasn't going to be fatal. I figured if I drew blood he'd take me seriously and answer my question.

Without moving his feet even an inch he raised his right hand and met mine at the wrist. He guided my strike down and away from his face. The defense had the grace of a dance move. He could have grabbed my wrist and broken it, or judo flipped me. He could even have turned the knife on me. I believed he was that capable.

He'd guided my arm and blade like a tai chi maneuver but sped up by like, fifty times. I hop-slid back to my first position and stared in what I'm sure was awe.

"Did you learn anything?" he said. "Just now?"

With a sigh, I eased Norma back into the scabbard. But only because intuition said he was being truthful about me not being his target.

"Look, Teddy, you can do whatever the fuck you want with Kyle. No tears here. But I'm begging you, don't do whatever it is you guys are going to do to the sheriff. And know that although this is a small-assed town, if you kill that lawman, you'll have the entire state and Feds on your ass so...."

"Where's the first place you'd look?"

"He's not at his home."

"Try again. Where...is the first...place you'd look?"

"His house but—"

He smiled briefly, which caused me to shut the door on my words.

"Like I said, you were always nice to me, Chloe. It meant a lot."

He pivoted so quickly, I nearly went for Norma Jean. He was out the door before my brain processed what the hell was happening.

Chapter Twenty-Six

The second Teddy left, I called the sheriff. No surprise, the call went straight to voicemail. I left a message anyway. Next, I called Raven Tawanna. Even though the first place she looked for the sheriff was his home, I believed Teddy. They must have had him at the motel or some other location and then moved him back home.

Maybe Arlo thought it was a clever hide-in-plain-sight type deal. Or maybe killing the sheriff in his own home would be some sort of twisted poetic justice. I really had no idea. I don't think like psychopaths. Still, I decided to trust Teddy's words.

Tawanna's phone went to voicemail as well. Her phone was turned off. Why? My breathing ticked up. Had she found him and they got the drop on her? I couldn't see it. These clowns weren't good enough to take Boulder and Tawanna, no chance.

But then I remembered how they got Sheriff Boulder. It had to be a fast-acting narcotic or something. But I told Deputy Tawanna my thoughts on that so she'd be on high alert.

"So why did it go to fucking voicemail!" I shouted at my phone.

I called my boss and told him I had an emergency and was going to lock up and leave. He was none too pleased. I didn't care. I broke all of Bucksville's posted speed limits driving home. My house was on the way to Sheriff Boulder's. I wanted to stop at home for two more knives. Maybe three. The whole drive, I wrestled with calling the cops from Moreford or going straight to the F.B.I. 911 line, if such a thing existed. But I remembered Jesse Arlo said no outside help or the sheriff would die. The closer I got to home the more freaked out I got.

I locked my brakes up and skidded to a stop just before my bottom step. I threw the driver's door open and leapt out, leaving the truck running. I cleared the three front steps and ran into the dark house. I turned a few lights on as I moved to my bedroom. I already had Norma Jean and the girl. I decided to go with my Gerber folding knife for my boot and one other knife.

Jeremiah Frank Savannah was a member of the united states marine corps. He bounced between Iraq and Afghanistan several times as a stop-loss soldier. He fought from two-thousand one to two thousand seven. In May of two-thousand ten, he took his life by way of his personal weapon, an M1911, also known as the Colt 1911. He was my father, my daddy. I was five years old when he died. As I said earlier, Momma sold his guns and she also sold his personal USMC issued OKC 3S military bayonet or knife. She sold it to a local trucker named Johnny Wheeler. When I had enough money saved, I tracked Johnny down and asked to buy the knife back.

He balked at first and had several questions as to why I wanted the knife so bad. I answered every question, determined that I would not leave his front porch without that knife in my possession. After a time, a big smile spread across his face.

"I'm satisfied with your answers, Chloe. The knife is yours."

I held out the money, but he refused.

"Your daddy fought for this country. I'm in his debt. I couldn't possibly accept money from his only daughter. I've kept the knife pristine, Chloe. It's kinda like I knew this day might come." He paused. A sad look came to his eyes. "I never should have purchased the knife. It's always belonged with your family."

I thanked him and went home. I never told Momma what I did. The knife has been hidden from her ever since. The blade is eight inches of 1095 carbon steel. The five inch leather bound handle makes her thirteen inches in total. It's a big weapon for a gal my size, but I put in the hours with the weapon, in case I haven't mentioned it. I also took the scabbard along with an old weight lifter's belt and forged a harness. I can wrap the belt around my waist and fit the knife upside down in the reconfigured scabbard. This way, the knife sits down on my back. A quick reach around and a significant downward jerk, the knife is free.

I pulled daddy's knife from the shoe box and fitted it in place. I was now officially ready for anything. Locked and loaded, I was good to go. I ran through the house and quickly locked the front door behind me. But something wasn't right. I scanned the yard—nothing. It was quiet. Why? What the—and that was it; my truck wasn't idling like I'd left it. The headlights were still on but dimming rapidly. I hopped in and tried to turn her over. She sputtered two times, then quit. Next three tries, she just made a clicking sound. Dead battery? Couldn't be. She was barely a year old.

Think Chloe, think.

The truck was running and then died. Clearly, the battery was dead but—shit, the fading lights. Alternator! I turned the key over one position, and sure enough, the alternator icon flashed red. The alternator's job is to keep electricity flowing when the truck is running. If the battery called it quits, that means the alternator drained all of the stored power in the battery. Conclusion: alternator done, thus, I was fucked. I put my head down. My thick hair draped around my shoulders. I pounded on the wheel. The horn blew. I was all out of ideas, until...

Shayna!

* * *

"Shit, I'm sorry, Chlo, Lexi and I are down in Palm Springs. My parents sprung for an AirBandB for us—my graduation gift. We took my car but listen, if you want to grab Rusty, go ahead. Sounds like you need to make good time so—"

"Should I throw your custom Circle Y saddle on him?"

"He'll love that," she said. "You both will."

Shayna designed a custom saddle that was part trail riding and part racing saddle and had Circle Y company build it for her. It was lightweight, with a shallow sweat flap and a single slender flank strap.

"Being summer, you'll have the light for a good while."

"And it promises to be clear with a near-full moon tonight, so visibility will be good," I said.

"I'm still not sure about this. Are you positive you can't call the cops? It sounds way out of your league."

"It might be," I said. "But have you ever talked me out of something when my mind is set?"

"We both know the answer to that," she said. "Please, at least tell my parents what you're up to so if you...if you're gone too long, they can—"

"I will."

We were both quiet on our sides of the line.

Finally, "You're a lying bitch."

"I know. Say hi to Lexi. Love you."

"Oh god, I really don't like—"

I killed the call before I listened to the voice of reason and chickened out. It was time to move, not think.

I tucked my phone away and quickly visualized the route I'd take to Shayna's. I stepped out of the truck, closed the door and—

Wham!

Something like a baseball bat struck me in the face. I fell to the ground and heard a voice coming from above. It was male with a slight slur.

"Get up, bitch. Get up n get what's comin' to ya."

I blinked my vision clear and recognized Brett Teagan. The brother to the giant that attacked Momma and me. He must have parked his truck up the road otherwise, I'd have heard him approach. He reached down and lifted me by my jacket sleeves. I was off my feet a moment then brought back hard to the ground. The vibration ran up my calves. He pinned me against the truck.

"You killed my brother. You and that cop and your bitch mom," he said. Whiskey and cheap cigar smoke covered my face. He wrapped a hand around my throat and squeezed. With one hand on his hand, I moved the other to Norma Jean.

"Nuh uh, not this time."

He covered my hand with his and squeezed my hand around Norma's hilt.

155

I thought my fingers would break. Now my hand and throat hurt with equal measure. I didn't have much time. His grip on my throat was too much for me. I'd pass out soon for sure, or worse, he'd crack the bones of my windpipe. I flashed through all of the martial art and self defense videos I watched.

Remain calm. Slow the breathing of what little breath you have.

His eyes were bloodshot. I took my hand from his strangling hand and jammed my thumb into his eye socket. I dug deep like I was trying to remove the entire eyeball.

"Fuck," he shouted. He released the grip on my throat then smacked me hard in the head with a backhand. I fell to the ground choking and coughing. He bent over and worked a hand at his eye. He called me a bitch, again and staggered toward me. I crawled under the truck and nearly made it until I felt his grip around my ankle.

"Where you think yer goin'?"

He dragged me out. I immediately kicked upward and caught him under the chin with the heel of my boot. He staggered back a moment but then charged in and fell on top of me. His weight was unbearable. I was completely pinned. He put his gross, sweaty, drunk face to mine.

"I had your momma, and now I'm gonna have you. And don't worry," he said. "This is definitely gonna hurt!"

The moment he went for his belt buckle, the weight on me reduced slightly. It was all I needed. I thrust my hips up as high as I could. He was lifted up for a moment.

"Ooh, a bucking bronco. This oughta be fun."

He put his weight back on me. What he didn't realize was I wasn't trying to buck him off. In that split second, I was able to reach to the small of my back where I kept Daddy's knife. Brett had his belt buckle open and was fumbling with his fly. And that's when I changed the course of his future.

I thrust my torso up and plunged the knife under his chin. His eyes went wide as a grotesque gurgling sound escaped his mouth. Blood spilled onto my face. He fell to the side, and I rode him all the way, twisting and turning the blade feverishly.

"You're done, asshole. But take pride because this here is a Marine's blade.

CHAPTER TWENTY-SIX

Semper Fi." I spat on him. "Say hi to your brother…bitch!"

I rolled off and took the blade with me. More blood spurted from the wound. He clutched at his throat and convulsed like a drowning man. I wiped the blood off on my jeans and felt something like joy as I watched him die.

Chapter Twenty-Seven

With daddy's OKC 3S sheathed, Norma at home, The Girl folding knife in my pocket, and my Gerber in my boot, I was barreling down the trail to Shayna's. My breathing was labored yet I was barely a quarter-mile into the trek. I figured it must have been the adrenalin. Once again I was willing my breath to slow. I was on a downward slope. I was tempted to haul ass but the ground had loose dirt with some large rocks. If I rolled an ankle I'd be of no use to Boulder or anybody.

I came to the bottom of the run and prepared to vault up the slope on the other side. I lengthened my stride and pumped my arms. My lungs complained but I pushed and pushed. Once at the top of the hill it would be a straight half-mile sprint-jog to Shayna's.

I closed in on the summit, and just before cresting the top, my left foot found loose dirt. My leg kicked out behind me. I fell face first and barely managed to slam my forearms down on the ground, which saved me from losing my front teeth—another lesson learned from my videos. It was something they called the 'break fall.' My arms screamed in pain, but at least I wouldn't need dental work.

The moon was in position to light up the earth as soon as the sun called it a day. I gave it everything I had as I moved across the open pitch. Shayna's sprawling mansion loomed up ahead. I got that feeling one feels when at sea, and land seems to get further away the closer you get. I knew it was just a trick the eye played and increased my speed. Pretty soon, Rusty would be doing all the heavy lifting. And then after that...

* * *

"Good god Chloe you're a mess. What happened?" Shayna's mother stood in the doorway in riding pants and boots with an Aztec blanket wrapped around her shoulders.

"Huh?"

"You're face is covered in blood. Are you hurt?"

"Oh no Mrs. Evans this isn't mine," I said fitting the custom saddle onto Rusty's back.

"Shayna said you'd be coming but she was being quite vague. And whenever she's like this, and it involves the two of you it's never good."

"Oh, it's nothing. Well, it's important but nothing dangerous." I forced a smile.

She crossed her arms across her body. "Neither one of you are any good at lying."

She tried to give me a stern look but we'd known each other long enough for me to catch a glimpse of a smile beneath the look. With a sigh, she hung the blanket up on a hook and walked over to Rusty and me. She stroked Rusty's neck and mane.

"It's nice you and Shayna have reconnected."

"I agree."

"Especially since you'll soon be traveling the world forgetting about us little people in Bucksville."

"Does everybody know everything about everybody?" I asked.

"You were raised here," she said. "You know the answer to that."

Rusty bobbed his head up and down and scratched at the hay on the floor.

"Well, Mrs. Evans."

"Yup, Rusty's getting a little restless. You better go."

After a brief hug, I walked Rusty out of the stable. Outside the door I mounted him and we were off. I promised Shayna's mother we'd both come back in one piece. Her brow furled in typical motherly fashion. In all honesty, I didn't know what shape I'd be when all was said and done. I'd keep Rusty safe though, that was for sure.

Together we galloped out over the plain. The wind pressed my hair back behind me. I came up in the stirrups and leaned in behind Rusty's neck. His stride stretched out as if to say 'thank you, now let's haul ass!' The moonlight cast plenty of light over the sandy terrain. We moved at breakneck speed toward the copse of trees.

"We gotta take it easy on the trail Rusty. No showing off." I convinced myself he not only understood the command but he'd also obey it. I was surprised I was able to feel my phone vibrate in my inside pocket. It would have to wait.

We got to the trail. I brought the gait down, and Rusty complied. We moved quickly but nowhere near full gallop. It wasn't safe at that time of day. We arrived at the creek near where Sheriff Boulder liked to fish. Rusty's hooves splashed into the water. We bolted across the creek. I hugged him tight as we vaulted up the bank on the other side. This put us on a different trail. Rusty began panting but showed no signs of wanting to rest.

Five minutes later, Boulder's house came into view. I pulled Rusty to a stop. He took the moment to hunt for grasses. I remembered my phone rang and checked it. It wasn't Tawanna or Boulder. Dang it! I didn't recognize the number, so I put the phone away.

"Let's get a little closer," I said and clicked my teeth. We maintained a walking pace. After about a hundred yards, I found the 300. The kidnappers did a piss poor job of stringing branches over the vehicle in an attempt to hide it.

City slicker losers.

As we got closer I saw Raven Tawanna's unit parked off near the back of the house. But before that, I noticed someone standing eighty yards out front of the house. It was too late to turn back or try to hide an eleven-hundred-pound thoroughbred. We were totally exposed thanks to the open ground and bright moonlight. I had an idea.

"Bear with me, boy," I said to Rusty. "Steady, keep it steady. Good boy."

As we neared the slender man, I recognized his voice from the incident at the Horse and Buggy. He spoke on a cell phone with his back to us. I leaned forward and onto the right side of Rusty's neck. We looked like a horse with a passed-out rider on top. Carter, the number two of Jesse's gang voiced ticked up when he noticed us.

"Hang on a sec. I'm doing first watch, and there's some fuckin'—What the fuck? Hey, hello? You. Rider. Hey!"

Rusty maintained his non-threatening gait.

"Hang on, Rolly, I gotta call you back."

We got within fifteen yards.

"Hello?" He called to us. I popped my head up and put my boot heels to Rusty's mid-section. "Hyaa! Punch Rusty!" It was a command I'd come up with for Rusty ages ago, which essentially meant—accelerate! In his heyday, Rusty's top speed was around fortyto forty-three miles per hour. Ain't nobody I know can draw his weapon fast enough in the ground Rusty needed to cover.

The man shouted, "Hey!" And attempted to draw his weapon. Rusty's barrel chest collided with the man. He flew straight back…and then directly under us. I glimpsed part of his face as he went down. The eye not covered by his long hair had terror in it. The gun blasted but the shot went wild. I turned Rusty around and doubled back. I didn't know what shape the man would be in. I was prepared to hop off Rusty and finish him with Norma Jean but there was no need. The first pass had done the trick. The side of the man's skull was caved in like a crushed coconut. Parts of brain matter actually glistened in the moonlight. The in-tact part of his face wore a clown-like expression of disbelief. The round he'd fired off must have been a dying reflex. Good riddance.

The shot would have been heard for certain. I hopped off Rusty and scooped up the dead man's gun. I mounted Rusty and had him at a gallop in seconds flat. I moved him out wide around the back of the house. Once I found vegetation thick enough, I tied Rusty up.

"I'll be back, Rusty. Good boy." I pet him vigorously and whispered more assurances. He'd done more than his part. I could not put him any further into harm's way. Shayna would kill me if she knew the stunt I'd pulled and I wouldn't blame her.

The henchmen known as Carter was off the table. That left Blocker, the big man nearly as big as Sheriff Boulder, and Jesse the boss. I hoped and prayed that Teddy, the Quiet One, was truly out of the game. This meant he was off to exact some sort of macho vengeance on Kyle. But if he was gone from this fiasco, good for Boulder, Tawanna, and me. In short, even with Teddy and Carter gone I was far from done. I just hoped my luck would hold.

I took a knee and checked the gun I took off Carter. It was a Beretta M9. And naturally, the guy had a custom pearl grip painted up to resemble desert camouflage.

What a douchebag!

I engaged the safety and checked the magazine. From the weight and peering into the witness hole, it was apparent the guy hadn't been fully loaded. With the spent round meant for me and Rusty and gaging the rounds I could see, plus the weight, I figured I had about eight rounds of the possible sixteen left. Returning the magazine home, I stood silently, still hidden by the trees.

The big dufus known as Blocker came out onto the porch and called out for Carter. He bellowed three times, throwing his voice in three different directions before giving up and retreating back inside. My guess was that while he was outside, Jesse would be inside keeping an eye on Boulder and more than likely Raven. With the gun in a two-handed grip, I sprinted to the rear side of the house. I pressed my back to the wall near Boulder's guest bedroom.

I took three deep, slow breaths, then peeked through the window. The bedroom was dark, but the bedroom door was open and gave me a clear sight of both Boulder and Tawanna. They were both bound at the ankles and hands behind their backs and sat on the living room floor. The sheriff and deputy were both beat up pretty bad. But so was Jesse, who held an ice pack to his face.

Boulder must have come to after the initial kidnapping, and Jesse got within striking distance.

Atta boy, Sheriff.

I ducked low and crept to the next bedroom, which was the sheriff's. I repeated my deep breaths and eased my head up for a decent look. I nearly leaped backward when I saw Blocker's wide back sitting on the bed. He was cursing and trying to fix a makeshift sling over his shoulder. I wondered who did that to him, Boulder or Raven Tawanna. I noticed he also had a handkerchief tied around his thigh. That was courtesy of me and Norma Jean at the Horse and Buggy.

My head must have cast a shadow, or maybe the guy had a sixth sense because suddenly, he jerked his head around.

"Fuck," he said. Our guns came up at the same time. I fired off a quick three-round burst.

Bam, bam, bam.

Glass shattered. He fell or jumped from his spot. A round from his gun hit the window frame, inches from my head. I jumped backward and fell hard on my tailbone. I scrambled backward in a crab walk as fast as my arms and legs would take me. One of his giant arms plopped out of the broken window frame. He hauled himself up but he was laboring.

"Kevlar bitch," he shouted and fired in my direction. My gun hand screamed in pain as the gun flew from my hand. It bled immediately. I gathered my feet under me and ran around the other side of the house out of firing range.

I leaned against the house breathing heavily. My hand was bleeding, but luckily I hadn't been shot. The bullet struck the gun and the force of the gun flying free, cut my hand near my thumb. The shitty news was I'd only fired three non-fatal shots and was now without a gun. On top of that, I hit the guy center mass as taught, but he was wearing Kevlar.

Kevlar, invented by a woman but protecting an asshole! Irony.

And so I was down to my knives, which wasn't all bad because I'm built for the weapon. I built myself up one throw at a time on the daily. I'm not bragging. Preparation is not bragging. I'm sure Serena Williams doesn't talk about how many practice serves she does in a year, or Valentina Shevchenko, the one hundred twenty-five pound mixed martial art champion count her practice roundhouse kicks. No, they just do. I just do. We're no different. In addition to all of the varieties of throws I mentioned earlier, I also throw my knives through the main rotations. No spin, half spin, and full spin. Both hands, as I mentioned before. I was about to go up against men, hard men. They'd for sure think they had the advantage because I'm a girl. They'd be wrong.

Underestimate me all you want, assholes.

They also have no idea about my knife skills. There's my advantage again. So, was this mixed-raced high school senior going to a gunfight with a knife? You're damn right, I was!

"Hey, little girl," Jesse called in a sing-song nursery rhyme voice. "Why don't you come inside and play?"

He was calling from the front porch, which meant they didn't know where I was. I ripped a section of shirt from my wool shirt and tied it around my hand. Boulder's log home sat on a raised foundation. I hauled open an access hatch and squeezed underneath. I belly crawled all the way to the far side of the house. I didn't dare exit near where Blocker and I had the shootout, as much as I wanted the gun back.

I reached the far access and froze. I listened intently. Movement in the house was minimal. Jesse kept on.

"You're never gonna save these two little girl. What are you anyway a high schooler?" He laughed at his comment. I was pretty sure he was trying to distract me while Blocker searched for me. But would he go window to window since they had captives inside or would he hunt outside on foot? I waited. I peered as best I could through all access grates. I never once saw Blocker.

"Say darlin' what'd you do to my boy Carter? He seems to be missing. And that Teddy fuck, ya seen him around?"

Thank god, Teddy was officially out of the game. I waited until Jesse ran out of things to say. I heard his footsteps on the porch followed by the front door closing. I eased out of the access grate. I stood and pulled Norma Jean and daddy's blade. We all know what they say about bringing knives to a gun fight but these guys were injured and I'm ridiculously practiced at throwing knives…in case I hadn't mentioned it. Get me in that room and I believed I could take them.

My deep breathing done a third time, I crept to the front of the house and eased onto the porch. I moved painfully slow easing my weight into each step as if adding grains of sand to a scale. I eventually made it to the front door. I listened. Nothing. I reached for the door handle. But as I did the door flew open. I was face to face with Jesse. I brought Norma up but was too slow. Jesse front kicked me square in the chest.

I staggered backward before falling down the five steps to the ground. The wind flew out of my lungs. I fought to catch my breath. I still had my knives. Jesse stood over me with a mocking grin plastered to his face.

"I knew you'd show up sooner or later. Now then." He raised his Glock and pointed it me. I was flat on my back but I wasn't going without a fight. Daddy would never approve if I did. I raised Norma up but barely got her a foot off the ground when Jesse was knocked clear over me. Deputy Raven Tawanna was still tied up. She'd hopped, somehow soundlessly to our spot and thrown her body into Jesse. The two of them hit the ground not far from me. I crawled as fast as I could move.

Deputy Tawanna lay crosswise over Jesse. She swung her head sideways and down with incredible speed and head butted Jesse square in the nose. I was almost to them. Jesse was dazed. He fumbled for his gun but by then I was on them.

"Move, Raven!" I shouted. She rolled off and to the side. Without hesitation, I lunged forward and dragged Norma Jean's blade across Jesse's throat. Blood spurted at least five feet in the air. He rolled to his side, clutching his neck with both hands. Raven rolled to her side, slid her hands down the back of her legs, and scooted her hands over her feet. She then ball-rolled onto her back and hopped straight to her feet. It was a move I'd only seen martial artists and gymnasts do. And it was called a kip up.

I cut her hands loose with Norma Jean and let her keep the knife to cut her feet loose. I bolted for the house and up the stairs.

"Chloe! Wait goddammit!" she called after me.

I burst through the door. Boulder was mid-stride, hopping toward Blocker. The sheriff slammed his shoulder into Blocker, who then stumbled into a Morris chair. With a loud thud, Blocker hit the floor. He got to a knee and raised his gun, aiming it toward Sheriff Boulder.

"Hey, Blocker!" I shouted. He turned toward my voice. By that time, Daddy's OKC 3S was halfway to him in the air. The blade sailed faster than anyone's eye could track. It only needed to travel eight feet. As the blade dove into Blocker's right cheek, his gun went off twice. The rounds splintered the hardwood floor at his feet. He remained upright as he clutched at the knife, which had penetrated between his lower jaw and the roof of his mouth. Blood poured from his mouth down his chin and from the entry wound. Still the man had fight in him. He teetered back, which meant I had to alter my position. I dove sideways over the coffee table, and that was when everything slowed down.

I must have been in what some call the zone. I'd unleash The Girl with a sidearm toss, half spin of the blade with thumb on top. I'd hit the coffee table, and momentum would carry me to the floor, where I'd have to cover my head before smacking into Boulder's grand hutch. I saw this future, all of it, in under a tenth of a second.

I leaped into action. Tawanna shouted something, but I blocked it out. I let The Girl go. It sailed until it found its home in the side of Blocker's neck. He tumbled backward in what seemed like slow motion. Blood spurted from his neck and cheek like a two-spigot fountain. Blocker was dead by the time his body hit the floor. After crashing onto the coffee table as visualized, I slammed onto the floor. Both arms sheltered my head a split second before I smacked into the hutch—elbows, and forearms first. I was going to be all right. I was in pain, but all right.

Raven rushed over and helped me to my feet.

"Jesus, Chloe," she said, looking at the dead man and blood spatter.

"Ain't no way I was hittin' Kevlar this time," I said. My legs went wobbly. The deputy caught me and helped me into a chair. She checked on Sheriff Boulder who seemed more pissed off than hurt. He came and stood over me.

"You saved our asses, kid. Thank you," he said. We stared at the dead man. Boulder didn't seem phased by the growing pool of blood on his floor.

"Your daddy would have been proud, Chloe, real proud."

"I know you guys have to do that evidence gathering stuff, but I'm going to need those knives back. Norma Jean, The Girl and daddy's.

Tawanna put a hand on my shoulder. "Your daddy's knife is your knife now, kid. You might wanna name her."

I thought about it a moment and decided I'd call her Marilyn. After that, my thoughts jumped to Rusty. I told the sheriff and deputy I was going to go pick him up.

"Rusty and I will be right back," I said. As I turned for the door, my phone buzzed.

"Really? Now?" Tawanna said and rolled her eyes.

It was the same number I hadn't recognized from earlier, but now with a slightly clearer head, it came to me.

"Doctor Griffiths, hi. Is Momma all right?"

"Chloe, I've been trying to reach you, the sheriff, everybody. Finally I—"

"Hang on, Doctor, slow down. I'm here with the sheriff and Deputy Tawanna and you're on speaker now."

"Oh shit, Chloe, I'm so sorry, but there's been an accident."

"Accident? What—"

"An attack actually. Chloe, a man by the name of Brett Teagan came to the hospital, and he...I'm afraid your mother's dead. He—"

The doctor started crying. "He killed her, Chloe. She's gone. I'm so sorry. He also badly injured a nurse on his way out. I was so worried about you because he ranted about making you and Deputy Tawanna pay as well and...oh my god, are you okay?"

"Yes, yes, and he won't...he can't...I killed him."

I handed Raven my phone as I felt my legs were going out on me again. Sheriff Boulder took over the call. Raven went to the kitchen and got me a glass of water. I took a huge guzzle.

Raven Tawanna, with eyes full of pity and business, asked, "Chloe, did you really kill Brett, the giant's brother?"

I nodded. I think.

"What a fucking day you've had." She wrapped her arms around me.

"Shit!" I said, shrugging her off. "Rusty! Rusty is tethered out behind the house about thirty yards. Can you call Shay—Shayna's parents and...horse trailer—"

"I'll take care of it," I think I heard Raven say.

A warm calm spread over me. And then everything went starless-night black.

Chapter Twenty-Eight

I buried Momma eight days after that fateful night. One thing I have to say about Bucksville is the amount of love I received from the people was humbling. It's a combination of good people meets 'it's our little town against the world.' Either way, I was touched. Nearly the whole town flanked me as I stood over Momma's grave. As for the townsfolk that couldn't make it, they sent love through cards, flowers, and food to the house.

I didn't bother with a wake or anything like that back at the house. And not because the house was too small, I just wanted to toss a handful of dirt on my Momma's casket and move on. Rather than have her spirit float around the wake eavesdropping on well wishers, I wanted to send her on to her reunion with daddy A.S.A.P. Sheriff Boulder, Shayna and Raven stayed close throughout the memorial service. My support team in the event my brain became dismantled or if I pitched over with a broken heart.

God love 'em.

At the close of pastor Daniel's service, I received hugs, kind words, and a few short reminiscences, all of which dated back to Momma's pre-drinking days. Who said what, about when, I have no recollection. I also can't recall how long I stood there before peeling myself away and moving toward Shayna's Mini Cooper wagon.

Phase two of the day was already set. Lexi drove while Shayna and I sat in the back seat. She held my hand in both of hers and offered soothing words each time I broke down. Lexi remained silent while she drove.

Before I knew it, the Cooper's tires were rolling over the paver stones of Shayna's roundabout. She and Lexi went up to Shayna's room to change while I used one of the downstairs guest rooms. We met back at the stables. To my surprise Lexi was still in the dress she wore at the service.

"Aren't you coming with us?" I asked.

"Nuh-uh, I think you and Shay need to—like—I've got stuff I gotta—"

"Thank you, Lexi," I said barely managing to croak it out. I gave her a tight squeeze. Shayna was already mounted on J.T. I put my left boot into the stirrup and hauled myself onto Rusty and followed my bestie out of the stable. We kept the horses at an easy stroll. It was as if Rusty read the vibe, because the retired racehorse made no attempt to take on J.T. as usual. Shayna and I hardly spoke as we moved over the low brown thirsty grass. It was exactly what I needed, and Shayna knew it…as always.

We reached our regular odd shaped giant live oak and dismounted. Sitting side by side with shoulders touching we soaked up nature's sights, sounds, and fragrances in silence. Shayna went for a dandelion in the same moment I grabbed a stick and worked it with Norma Jean. Our routine was so simple and easy that without it, in that moment I might have shattered into a thousand pieces.

"You buy your ticket yet?" Shayna asked. I don't know where I'd drifted but her gentle voice guided me back to shore.

"Yeah, I, uh, leave in a couple weeks. I've got a flight to Heathrow, and from there, I'll get my ass to either Spain or Italy. I haven't decided which yet."

"I think this will be good for you, Chlo."

"I think so," I said. "Hope so anyway."

"So what about the house?"

"Geraldine's sister Lila runs a rental agency."

"Yup, she and her husband," Shayna said.

"If I decide to stay longer than a month or two, she says she'll find me a tenant, or we'll set it up as an AirBnB. We'll set up an account that I can access from there, and then—"

Shayna looked away briefly then came back. "My god, I can't believe you're doing this. I'm happy-sad for you."

Yes, we hugged again. I'm sure you're gagging by now with all of the tears and hugs but, it's my story so…

"Dang girl," Shayna said, easing backward. She pulled a thin hair out from between her lips. "I'll miss you, Chlo, but I swear to god I'm not gonna miss that long ass hair of yours. Are you ever gonna cut it?"

"Yeah right, you'd just love for me to get a boyish pageboy cut with some ugly ass bangs, wouldn't you? You are so effing jealous."

"Jealous, ha? Your shit's a mess," she laughed.

"Maybe I should thin it out," I said. "Like yours."

Shayna let out her famous cackle. The sound made my heart shatter into a trillion pieces. It was my favorite sound. A sound I cherished even more than the sounds of nature. I'd miss Shayna's cackle more than anything else in Bucksville.

We slipped back into silence for another five minutes or so.

"Look, Chloe, I haven't been totally honest with you. Well, I haven't lied or anything, but there's something I haven't told you."

I turned to her but she kept her eyes on the dandelion.

"When you and I ended—when I ended our friendship," she stopped and let the dandelion fall from her hands and wiped at her eyes.

"When I left you it wasn't because of Momma's drinking. Not entirely anyway."

She took in a huge gulp of air and pushed on. "Something happened one summer. The last summer we hung out."

"Yeah, we were like eleven, and my uncle came out," I said.

"Right. So do you remember the day you went for takeout from Geraldine's? I didn't have my bike with me, so you went on your own."

"Uh-huh," I said, nodding. Shayna's body began to stiffen, and her words came out clipped and jerky.

"I stayed back with Momma and her brother, your uncle Clive." Tears began to flow, but this time, she let them roll down her cheeks.

"At first, it was nice. We laughed and acted all goofy. But then Momma said she was going to take a short nap."

She stopped there and squeezed her eyes shut. I put a hand on her knee and gently rubbed. My temples got hot. I've had a lifetime of experiences with men and I knew where this was going better than I knew my own name.

"And then your uncle, he…he paid me like these fucking compliments and—"

"Oh fuck, did he rape you, Shayna? Did he?"

"No, no, Chloe, he didn't," she gasped. "He tried. He came at me and my shirt ripped," she let out a huge breath. "Anyway, I screamed, and Momma came running, thank god! She took a saucepan and went to town on that bastard. Sorry, but he deserved it."

"No shit, he did!" I said. My own tears were flowing now but they were the angry kind.

"I didn't stick around. Momma was still beating on him when I ran outta there. I ran all the way home without looking back once."

I jerked Norma Jean and thrust her into the ground with a loud 'fuck!' The horses stirred.

"I realize now that when I never looked back I was leaving Momma, your uncle, and you, all of you behind," her voice dropped to a whisper. "And look at us now."

My breathing ramped up. I wanted to plunge my knives into every son of a bitch on the planet. Norma, The Girl, all of them would never work so hard and would be an unrecognizable red when I was done. Why was I never told about this! Shayna's voice brought me back from my would-be killing spree.

"I was so freaked out, ya know. I don't know much about what happened next, but I know my parents got Sheriff Boulder involved, and Momma—"

Her words trailed off. I couldn't take this on the day I'd buried my mother. My heart felt like it would push through my ribs until it exploded. Something clicked, and I realized I was making it about me and not my best friend who just unloaded a bombshell on me. Or rather, off her chest!

"I'm so sorry," I said, pulling her into a hug. The horses, sensing our energy, stirred some more. I shh'd them as much as Shayna as she cried into my breast.

When we pulled apart I yanked Norma out of the dirt and cleaner her off on my jeans. Back into the sheath she went.

"I wanna kill my uncle," I blurted. "So what finally happened to the asshole?"

"I was so messed up I refused to go back to school. I thought when word got out, which it would, I thought in this town—"

"So that's why you home schooled," I said.

She nodded.

"I am so—"

"Stop apologizing, Chloe. You didn't do anything wrong."

"So what about Boulder and my uncle and…."

Her eyebrows went up in a 'holy shit' expression. Whenever this happened when we were kids, it meant a big time story was coming.

"Never mind, Boulder, but your girl officer Bad Ass, as you call her, went totally nuts. She got hold of your uncle and beat him so bad he spent seven months in hospital. Seven fucking months, Chlo!"

Shayna sat forward and crossed her legs under her.

"It took both Boulder and Burris to pull her off. She would have killed him otherwise."

"Fuck me," was all I could manage.

"I know, right?"

"Was my sleazeball uncle ever charged with sexual assault?" said the ever hopeful friend.

She sighed. "No, because he lawyered up and went after Tawanna for assault and police brutality all that stuff. So Jim Boulder ended up as like, a mediator. He kept Tawanna out of jail, and she kept her job, while your uncle—"

"Uncle Asshole."

"Yes, Uncle Asshole, uh, walked…once he was able," she said with a giggle.

Silence crept in again while Shayna allowed me to digest. I twirled Norma Jean around a few times, then put her in the sheath. I didn't want to freak the horses out.

"Pedophile uncle, drunk mother, and Daddy—" Tears threatened again but I beat them back. I eased Norma Jean back out. I found a flat stone and began to sharpen her. Shayna gave me the time. I moved the blade over the stone a good twenty or thirty times. Testing the blade with my fingers, I gently slid her back into her home.

"Any idea where my uncle is today?" I forced myself to sound as casual as if asking about the day's weather.

"Um yeah, oh my god, last I heard he's in Italy."

Shayna's face turned ashen. "Oh, Chloe, no, I know that look. Don't you—let sleeping dogs lay, ya hear me."

"From Heathrow, I'm heading to Italy," I said calmly.

"No...you're...not."

I stood and untied Rusty. "Last one home's a total loser." I grinned but wasn't particularly happy.

"Rusty! Hyaaa! Punch!"

Epilogue

I t had been two months since Momma's funeral and my last ride with Shayna. Of all the potential murders I could have been charged with: Brett Teagan, Carter, Blocker, and Jesse Arlo, I was cleared of each one. In fact, there wasn't even a trial. Everyone from Boulder to Shayna, Officer Bad Ass, and back again wanted me to attend grief counseling. As well as counseling after having killed people. I assured all concerned parties that I had it covered. After everything that went down that week, I was totally spent. I barely had the energy to attend my graduation and only did so because I know Momma, and daddy for that matter, would have wanted me to go.

Since then, I've been taking the grieving process on my own, one day at a time over the loss of Momma. As far as the potential for me undergoing PTSD, I've been keeping an eye on it—whatever that means. I had a lengthy talk with Sheriff Boulder and deputy Tawanna. They pretty much confirmed what Shayna told me about my slime ball uncle Clive. After a thousand assurances, my trip to Europe was for grieving and therapy, and that there was barely a sliver of anger left in my heart, they bid me farewell... but not goodbye.

Italy turned out to be more beautiful than I ever expected, even though I'd done the research. Research can't relay just how friendly and beautiful the people are. A perfect stranger inviting you into their home for a meal is not a rare occurrence. The adage they work to live not live to work is true. And darned near everyone from a baker to a professor has a beautiful singing voice and can burst into song seemingly without reason. Italy's beauty and charm managed to soften the edges of my intent on revenge on my uncle. In truth, I didn't really know what I'd do if I found him beyond some sort of confrontation. But now, two months into my trip, I barely thought of Uncle Clive. He wasn't worth my thoughts. In addition to that…

"Another espresso, belina?"

"No, grazie, Salvatore."

"Bene, anything else?"

"I was eyeing that cannoli in the case," I said.

"Coming right up. But now in Italian, per favore."

"Un cannolo per favore, Salvatore."

"Ah," he clapped his hands. "Tuto bene!"

"Grazie."

Salvatore flashed his gorgeous smile and headed off the get my dessert. Part of what made his smile so ridiculous was his deep blue eyes. A beautiful color on their own, but at the outer corners they had light flecks of teal. So that covered the color, but they were also the kindest eyes I'd seen in a long time. My guess is he was about twenty or twenty-one, which was fine with me being as girls mature faster than boys, right?

His body was perfectly lean. By that I mean he was fit but looked like did just enough exercise to keep it tight. I can't stand guys that over-build their bodies with stupid bulging muscles. I swear they do that for other dudes anyway. Do I need to talk about his thick black, wavy hair? Nah, I think you get the picture. The boy was snack!

* * *

Oh, I almost forgot to mention: Teddy Watkins, the Quiet One. The night when my shit-show was in full effect, Teddy took the rental van they'd used to snag Boulder and disappeared. Two weeks later, I graduated. A day after that, Teddy drove to Kyle's home. He knocked on the front door, and both Kyle and his mother answered. Teddy told them who he was. Apparently satisfied that Kyle remembered him, Teddy grabbed Kyle and snapped his neck. Kyle's mother screamed in horror. Teddy hopped in the van and tried to blow town, but Kyle's mother pulled herself together long enough to call the cops. Specifically, deputy Bad Ass.

Raven Tawanna caught up with Teddy outside of Moreford. She waited for a turn in the road, pulled up close, and rammed his rear bumper. The van spun out of control. Teddy popped out of the van with his gun blazing. Tawanna took a round high on the chest while Teddy took three rounds inside the ten ring. Deputy Tawanna survived thanks to her Kevlar vest.

Kevlar. Designed by a woman. Protects a Bad Ass woman. Justice.

Teddy, on the other hand, was not wearing a vest. And although all three rounds went into his heart, it was probably bullet number one that stopped it. When I heard the news I sent Deputy Bad Ass a long distance two-word text.

Good Girl.

Her response, which came nine hours later was simple: it was the rock n roll hand sign emoji.

* * *

Salvatore, along with three other staff members, arrived with my cannoli.

"Grazie mille, Salvatore. What's going on?" I said looking at the group.

To my total shock the four of them launched into Tanti Auguri, the birthday song in Italian. I was so embarrassed. I hid my face in my hands until they were done. Patrons in the cafe applauded me.

"My god, how did you know it was my birthday, Salvatore?"

"The first time you came, I asked for I.D. when you used your card. It was-a-not necessary, I just wanted to see your birthdate. Today you are eighteen, no?"

"Si, and you are very cheeky," I said.

"Bon compleanno belina." He kissed me on both cheeks.

While his coworkers went back to work, Salvatore hovered. He was clearly waiting for me to taste the dessert.

"I don't usually eat this stuff," I said. "Not even from my friend's bakery back home."

"But this is-a Roma Bella mia."

"That it is. And you know what they say; when in Rome…."

I sunk my teeth into what was the most paradisiacal delight I'd ever tasted. My mouth exploded with a flavor out of this world.

"Fuck me!" I blurted.

"Scusa?"

"Oh, sorry," I said, laughing with a mouth full of goodness. "I meant to say, ah, deliziosi cannoli!"

Salvatore put his blue-teal eyes on me. A sly grin played at his soft lips. He pulled up a chair uninvited. I didn't protest.

"So tell me, Bella mia," he said with his sexy accent. "How long will you be here in-a-Roma?"

"I have no idea, Salvatore. I'm here to meet a family member."

"A capito, I understand."

"But I'm not looking that hard so I'm…kinda free…a lot."

"This is molto bene Bella mia. Molto bene!"

As I said earlier, I had sex once, and it was awful. And then there was the 'almost time' with Kyle. In that moment, when Salvatore put his eyes on me, I wanted to jump him, and soon. Everything was as close to perfect as could be. I was where I wanted to be, and with someone I was pretty sure was going to be the 'who' I wanted to be with.

But then, over Salvatore's shoulder, I saw him. His hair had flecks of gray, which was new, and he carried more weight around the middle. He stopped and chatted with a girl selling jewelry off of a folding table. The girl looked to be about my age. She laughed at something he said. The blood in my veins actually felt like it was heating up. A thousand memories flooded in. I realized I'd been a dormant volcano these past two months. Seeing him now, flirting with a girl far too young for him, I could feel the volcano was ready to erupt.

The man across the street was my mother's brother. My uncle Clive. The one who touched Shayna and would have done more if…

"What is it, belina?" Salvatore asked. His face full of concern.

"Famiglia."

"Ah, the family member you're looking for."

"Yeah, and I just found him," I said with a sigh. "I'll be right back."

Acknowledgements

I'd like to acknowledge the women and men in healthcare. They stood strong on the front lines through two-plus years of COVID, facing long hours, limited PPE, and health issues of their own. These tireless workers showed up day in and day out while most of us quarantined. Now with the virus on its heels, it's business as usual for our healthcare professionals—the business of saving lives. As I battle with multiple myeloma, a blood plasma cancer, I'd personally like to thank all healthcare professionals with a specific shoutout to the amazing staff at Kaiser Permanente. Thank you for keeping me in the fight!

About the Author

Jonathan Brown has written three books in the Lou Crasher mystery series: *The Big Crescendo, 2019; Don't Shoot the Drummer, 2020;* and *Drums, Guns N Money* pub date March 2023. He's written two books of historical fiction, both with favorable *Kirkus* Reviews. *A Boxing Trainer's Journey,* a novel based on the life of Angelo Dundee, and *Character Is What Counts* a novel based on the life of Vince Lombardi.

Chloe is his first book with a female protagonist and his first book with Level Best Books. Two more books with female 'bad ass' protagonists are underway and will be published with Level Best.

Brown is the first recipient of Mystery Writers of America's Barbara Neely Scholarship 2021. He's one of the founders of Sidecrow Productions, an audiobook production business. In addition to penning stories, Brown has added audiobook narration to his trick bag. For fun, he plays drums, practices martial arts, and messes around with simple carpentry projects. But most of all he enjoys love and laughter with his beautiful wife Sonia.

SOCIAL MEDIA HANDLES:
  Instagram: @JonathanBBooks

AUTHOR WEBSITE:
  www.jonathanbrownwriter.com

Also by Jonathan Brown

*Moose's Law…*A Doug 'Moose' McCrae Novel

The Lou Crasher Series
  The Big Crescendo
  Don't Shoot The Drummer
  Drums, Guns N Money

Non-Fiction
  A Boxing Trainer's Journey
  Character Is What Counts

www.ingramcontent.com/pod-product-compliance
Lightning Source LLC
Chambersburg PA
CBHW050334110726
47899CB00007B/2502